saving zasha

RANDI BARROW

SCHOLASTIC

Scholastic Children's Books
An imprint of Scholastic Ltd
Euston House, 24 Eversholt Street
London, NW1 1DB, UK
Registered office: Westfield Road, Southam, Warwickshire, CV47 0RA

First published in the US by Scholastic Inc, 2011
This edition published in the UK by Scholastic Ltd, 2011

ISBN 978 1407 12478 0

A CIP catalogue record for this book
is available from the British Library.

Printed in the UK by CPI Bookmarque, Croydon, Surrey
Papers used by Scholastic Children's Books are made
from wood grown in sustainable forests.

3 5 7 9 10 8 6 4 2

www.scholastic.co.uk/zone

To Arthur, for making it possible

PROLOGUE

"Mikhail! Someone's coming!" my brother, Nikolai, shouted, running into the barn. "Is she here?"

"No," I answered, barely breathing. "I just put her in the hiding place and came back to get some food."

The sharp, grinding sound of a vehicle on the gravel road at the front of our farm grew louder. A battered yellow van pulled to a stop and two men jumped out.

The driver, a heavyset man who looked like he had forgotten to shave, said, "Hello, boys," in a friendly way that I knew was not friendly at all. His passenger, a pale-eyed young man, carried a pole with a leather loop on the end. Nikolai and I stood still and silent. They walked through the open barn door uninvited.

"What do you want?" my brother asked, using his most grown-up voice. The driver didn't answer immediately. He walked slowly around the area where my father had built pens for the geese and the pigs, although it had been four years since we sold our last pig. It seemed very little escaped his attention. The man with the pale eyes stood quietly, but he, too, was looking closely at everything in our barn.

As casually as I could, I picked up a bucket of feed and walked to the goose pen. "Excuse me, it's their breakfast time." The driver reached out and grabbed my upper arm as I passed him, making me stop. I tried not to show my fear as I looked at his hand and then into his eyes.

"I understand you have a German shepherd here."

"You're wrong. May I?" I asked, looking towards the mother goose and her three little ones as if our conversation were over and I wanted to finish my chores. He let go of my arm.

"We have no dogs at all. Not since the year before the war started," Nikolai said. I was just two years younger than my fifteen-year-old brother, and together we had learned to lie well. Not because we were dishonest, but because Russia had been at war for four years and it was sometimes necessary to keep you out of trouble.

The man with the pale eyes stared hard at us, as if willing and ready to do whatever his companion told him to do. The driver lifted the lid of a grain storage box and peered in.

"Many dogs starved during the war," my brother

continued, which was unnecessary because everyone remembered how little food there had been and how many people and animals had died of hunger. The pale-eyed man looked at the driver as if to say, *These two are idiots; they have nothing to tell us*.

The driver ignored him, then stopped in the middle of the barn, hands on his hips. He looked up at the ceiling where slivers of light came in through the cracks between the planks of the roof.

"Why, I wonder, would anyone tell us lies about such a thing?"

My brother and I looked at each other and shook our heads, as if we couldn't imagine.

"Not just a dog," he said, looking at each of us as if we were confidants, "but a *German shepherd*. Very specific."

"Only traitors would keep a German shepherd," his companion said, practically shouting at us. "Or maybe you are traitors. Maybe you are hiding a German, and not just a German dog."

"Stop!" my brother yelled at him. "How dare you accuse us of such a thing! Our father was killed in the war – by Germans!"

"We're not sure he's dead, Nikolai," I said, angry that he would talk about our father in front of strangers. Even when it was just us together, we never talked about him as if he were gone for good. My voice got louder. "He could be in a prison camp or a hospital, or—"

"Settle down, boys," the big man snapped. To his partner he added, "Pavel, go wait in the van."

Now that Nikolai and I were alone with the driver, my hands started shaking. To stop him from noticing, I put down the feed pail without finishing the chore, walked to the wall where a rake rested, picked it up and began to tidy the hay on the floor.

"If you have a German shepherd, we will find him."

"We told you," I said. "We don't have a—"

"And when we find him. . ."

"We have no dog," my brother repeated patiently. "We would love one, my sister especially. The war was hard on us. We lost many things."

"Yes, well," he said with a sniffing sound a little like a laugh. "The war was hard on all of us." Clapping his hands together suddenly, he said, "All right. No dog here. But we'll be back. Just in case."

"Who are you?" my brother demanded.

"Who do you think we are?"

"The Red Army?"

"Do you see an army uniform?"

"No, but—"

"A dogcatcher?" I said. "Gypsies? Dog thieves? Show us your identification."

His eyes narrowed. "Here's my identification." He pulled his coat back to reveal a gun in a holster under his left arm. "And that's who I am. You figure out the rest." With one last, angry glance around the barn, he left.

As he climbed into his truck, he stood momentarily on the running board. "If you are lying, and I find the dog . . . well, let's just say there are labour camps that could use the help of two strong young boys such as yourselves. Out in the eastern provinces." He laughed as he said this last sentence. There was no laughing in my heart, because as everyone knew, few came back from Russia's eastern provinces.

"Come on, Yuri," his passenger called out, which finally got him in the van. They sped out on the narrow road, spewing dust and pebbles in their wake.

My brother and I, as if by agreement, collapsed on a bale of hay in the corner of the barn. "If they'd come earlier, they might have found her," I said, kicking at a wet lump of mud on the floor.

"I know," my brother replied softly, as if still recovering from the scare they gave us.

"How many German shepherds do you think have been killed by now?"

Nikolai looked at me, but seemed to be far away. "I

saw one shot in the street in Leningrad." He was visiting an aunt when the artillery bombardment began and barely made his way back home before the city was surrounded and one million died.

"But that was in the city, and the Germans bombed the people there. How many do you think they've killed here in the country?"

"All they could find."

"But the war is over now," I argued, "and I'm sure Zasha's never hurt anyone, and never would."

"It doesn't matter. Even though the Germans lost the war, people are angry that they started it. Did you hear that some people are even destroying cuckoo clocks?"

I laughed for the first time since the men arrived. "Because they're made in Germany? That's ridiculous. What's next – accordions? Nikolai . . . do you hate the Germans?"

"Yes, of course. . . I don't know. I've promised myself that if Papa comes home, I won't hate anyone ever again."

"I'm going to go see Zasha right now," I said, getting up, still chilled by the visit from the strange men.

"No! Wait until we're sure they've gone. They could be watching."

"But I know she's hungry, and—"

"If you want her to live, you must be clever. And patient."

CHAPTER ONE

Zasha had come to us only two weeks before the visit from the men in the yellow van. That clear Sunday morning, I'd ridden our horse, Paku, to the very edge of our land where it meets the forest. I was looking for a patch of wild clover I'd seen; it was Paku's favourite thing to eat. It was ironic that I had to search for one when our entire farm was supposed to be planted with clover this summer. It was a trick my father knew; after you grow flax for several years, you must stop for a season and grow clover. You bring in cows to eat the clover, they fertilize the soil with their droppings, and – miracle – the soil is rich again and you can go back to farming flax.

It hadn't worked out that way, of course. Our papa wasn't with us to watch over the officials who were supposed to supply us with the clover seed and the cows. But the good thing about not getting to plant clover was that our farm was quiet for a change, peaceful, free of the comings and goings common at this time of year.

I rode to the forest slowly, towards the line of shade made by pine, fir and birch. I let Paku stop whenever he wanted to have a bite of grass or a drink from one of the small streams that crossed our farm. It was late June and everything seemed like it was in bloom. I was happy just to ride Paku and spend our morning wandering.

Suddenly, a man stumbled out from behind a tree and grabbed tight to Paku's bridle.

"What do you want?" I could barely speak, I was so surprised and frightened.

"Help me," he said. I looked hard at him, trying to understand what he needed help with, when I saw the cut on the left arm of his coat, rimmed with blood.

"How?"

"I'm hurt. I need bandages, medicine, or it will become infected." I knew how easily a person could die from an infected cut; my mother reminded me of it constantly when Nikolai and I played in unfamiliar places.

"How did this happen?" I asked.

"A man tried to steal my . . . a man tried to steal something from me."

"What did he want?"

The man looked at me with eyes that seemed watery, or almost feverish. It made me think infection had already set in. "Are you alone?"

I didn't want to answer, and pulled Paku's reins slightly to the left. If he tried to hurt me or steal my horse, I could turn faster that way and he would fall.

"I'm sorry, I didn't mean to scare you. It's just that. . ." He closed his eyes and leaned his head against the side of Paku's head. "Can I trust you?" he asked suddenly, straightening up.

"Yes," I answered, more nervous with every passing moment.

He turned and whistled softly. Out of the darkness of the forest came the most beautiful German shepherd I had ever seen. Its coat was golden and lustrous, with black hair on its back and black markings on its face. "Someone tried to steal my dog. Zasha, come." The dog trotted forward and came to rest at his side.

It was the first time I'd seen a dog in years, and never one this exquisite; I was awestruck. "He's beautiful."

"She," he said. "Zasha."

Then this poor man who had made me so fearful suddenly crumpled into a pile on the ground. I was no longer afraid of him, but only of what might happen to him. I jumped off my horse. Zasha licked the face of her master rapidly; he groaned and managed to sit up.

"Can you help me?"

"Yes. Do you think you can get up on my horse?"

"I don't know." I helped him to his feet. He looked at the stirrups and shook his head, as if he didn't believe he had the strength to accomplish such a huge task.

"Come," I said in as bold a tone as I could manage, the one my father used with me when I needed to summon courage. I laced my fingers together, forming a step for him to put his foot in to boost him up and on to Paku. "You'll sit behind me and we'll be at our farm in no time."

He failed on the first attempt.

"Use all your strength. Push yourself up and swing your leg over. That's all you have to do." He looked at me doubtfully, but I saw a flash of determination pass over his face. On that attempt he made it; in fact, he almost slipped off the other side of Paku because he had put so much effort into it. I swung up easily after him.

"Hold on to me if you need to," I said as I turned Paku back in the direction from which we'd come. I felt the man lean against me, as an exhausted child might do. Without being told to, Zasha followed closely on our right. Paku didn't seem too happy about the extra load, but he accepted my lead and in a short time we were within sight of the farmhouse.

My mother was hanging out clothes on a rope strung between two trees so that they would dry in the sunshine. She stopped her work when she saw me. I could tell by the way she stood up straight and stared that she had seen the man and the dog with me and was wary, maybe even frightened. Her hand went into the pocket of her long, dark skirt. I knew she always kept a knife with her, a precaution she took since we lived on a secluded farm, and especially since my father left for war.

The weight of the man had grown heavier and heavier against me as we rode. I was afraid that if I dismounted first, he'd fall off Paku.

"Mama!" I cried as soon as I thought she could hear me. "I have a sick man with me. We have to help him."

She ran towards us, which was a good thing because I was pretty sure the man was unconscious given the way he was slowly sliding to the left. My mother lifted her hands up just in time to break his fall. I jumped off Paku and together we laid the man on the ground. Zasha was at his side immediately, disturbed and whimpering.

"Mikhail," she said sternly, "tell me what happened. And keep the dog away from him." I slipped my hand under Zasha's worn leather collar and dragged her a metre away. She was strong and determined to go no further.

"I met him near the forest. We were looking for clover and . . . he said someone attacked him. Look at his coat; it's cut and bloody."

My mother had become a less trusting person since my

father had left for the war. "How do you know it's true? He could be a thief, or a deserter or a madman."

"I know, Mama," I said softly, "but I don't think so." She must have sensed the same thing, because she began unbuttoning his jacket. He moaned in pain and awakened when she tried to ease him out of it to examine his arm.

When he opened his eyes and saw my mother's face, his expression was one of hope and relief. "Thanks be to God," he whispered. "Do you have . . . water?" He could barely get his words out.

She didn't answer immediately because she was examining his arm. The cut had gone through his coat and his shirt, deep into his arm.

"Who did this to you?" my mother asked.

"A man . . . a thief. Please help me."

"Why did he do it?"

"He wanted . . . he wanted. . ."

"Mother, please!" I interrupted. "It doesn't matter. Help him!"

My mother made a decision. "Nikolai!" she cried, looking back at the farmhouse. "Nikolai! Come quickly!"

He came running out of the back door, followed by my nine-year-old sister, Rina. When they reached us they stood as though in shock, gazing at the bloody, ailing man and the restless, anxious dog. "Where did you get that?"

Rina asked in a voice just above a whisper, pointing at Zasha.

Nikolai gazed from man to dog and back again, finally joining me, reaching out to touch the fur on Zasha's neck just as my mother said, "Boys – help me carry him into the house. We'll put him in the bedroom at the back."

Nikolai grabbed him under the shoulders, which caused the man to cry out. My mother and I each lifted one of his legs, and together the three of us managed to get him up four steps, into the house, and on to the narrow bed in the bedroom at the back. This was the room where workmen sometimes stayed when we had a particularly good harvest.

"Who is he?" Rina asked, as we stood transfixed by the barely conscious man on the bed.

"He is a man who needs help," my mother said. "Mikhail, get me scissors and bandages. Rina, put some water on to boil. Nikolai, go through his coat and his pockets and see if you can find some identification."

"Yes, Mother," we murmured as we began our tasks. I was back with scissors and bandages in seconds, and watched as my mother carefully snipped off the entire arm of his ragged shirt.

The cut was a savage, dirty red with a yellow liquid oozing from it. She shook her head. "His arm is badly infected. Go and see if Rina has the water ready." Soon, on the table next to the bed, sat two bowls of steaming water, soap and a tin of herbs my mother claimed cured everything from stomach aches to broken bones.

She dipped a cloth into the hot water and gently dabbed the cut on his arm. "First, we're going to clean you up," my mother told him. He winced as the warm cloth touched his skin, and opened his eyes.

"Water," he whispered.

"Mikhail. Bring me a small pitcher of water. There is whiskey on the top shelf in the kitchen. Bring that, too." It was then that I knew how serious his condition must be. The half-full bottle of whiskey sat untouched after my father left for the war. My mother always said we would drink the rest on the day he returned. Now we would offer it to a stranger to help save his life.

I brought the water and the whiskey and the small, thick glass from which my father liked to drink it. "Here," I said, offering them to my mother.

"Pour him some water," my mother instructed. "Add just a little whiskey. He might not be able to tolerate it." I did as she told me.

"Let me finish with the soap first," she said, as she tenderly stroked the area surrounding the wound. "There. Now, hold his head up and give me the glass.

"Here we go," she said to him gently. "I want you to drink this. Just a little at a time. It will help you feel better." The man let her place the glass to his lips and tried his best to drink. Much of the liquid poured out the sides of his mouth.

"That's good," she said, as if talking to a child. "Now I'm going to put medicine on your arm to see if we can clear up that infection." His head sank back on to the thin pillow. Nikolai and Rina stood at the foot of the bed, watching everything closely. Zasha sat between the two of them, eyes fixed on the face of her master. Both Nikolai and Rina patted the dog on her head and back as if they couldn't keep themselves from touching her.

"Mikhail, take the dog. Tie it up in the barn," my mother said.

"No!" the man cried, making what looked like an attempt to sit up to stop her from taking the dog from him, but succeeding only in causing a convulsion of pain.

"Shhh," she replied, looking almost alarmed at the vehemence of his response. She touched his uninjured arm gently. "The dog can stay."

My mother made a paste in the palm of her hand out of the dry herbs and a few drops of water. "This may sting just the slightest bit," she told the man, carefully smoothing the mixture up to the very edges of his wound.

He must have felt the sting because I saw his forehead tense up, but he said nothing.

"What's your name?" my mother asked.

"Petr," he answered, as if he could barely remember.

"I want you to take another drink of the water, Petr . . . that's it," she said, as he took another small sip. "And I want you to rest." She then gently wound the gauzy bandage over the deep cut in his arm. "In the morning we may have to stitch you up, but I think that's enough for now." He opened and closed his eyes as if to say he understood.

Throughout the day and into the night, my mother repeated the process of cleaning, applying herbs and bandages, and giving Petr whiskey and water. We children followed and watched. Zasha never left his side, no matter how many times we tried to get her outside for some fresh air.

Nikolai's search of Petr's coat revealed nothing but a few small coins and a button. I was always grateful that my mother thought to ask him his name.

It was the last word he spoke. Sometime in the night he passed away.

CHAPTER TWO

I was the one who found him. His face was so pale, and he was so still, that I knew he was gone. Zasha lay on the narrow bed next to him as if to warm him or give him comfort in his last minutes.

My mother entered the room; she put her hand on my shoulder and sighed. "His infection had gone too deep. Wake Nikolai. We'll have to take him to the village and explain."

"But, Mama – what about the dog?"

"The dog," she repeated in a tone that suggested she had been avoiding even thinking about Zasha.

"Look at her. She's a good dog, and clever, you can tell. Please, Mama, let us keep her!"

"We'll take her with us to the police station. She's not ours; we can't keep her."

I felt pressure building in my chest, like I couldn't breathe. "They'll kill her, Mama, you know they will. She's a German shepherd. Don't you remember? Nikolai saw people shoot them in Leningrad."

"No. There could be trouble. We don't need trouble." She turned to leave the room. Then I did something I had never done before – I dropped to my knees.

"I am begging you for the life of this dog, Mother. Please let us keep her. No one has to know."

"No," she said. I grabbed her skirt with my hands.

"Mother, please! We lost Papa, we lost all our other dogs, we lost. . ."

She closed her eyes and held up her hand as if to say *Stop!* I stayed still in the silence until she reached out her hands to draw me to her. I stood up and we hugged for a very long time.

"You've been so brave." I didn't answer, but thoughts of the soldiers we'd seen, the tanks, the guns, the sounds of fighting in the distance, all rolled through my brain. Almost everyone in our village had lost at least one family member.

"Is it against the law to have a German dog?" I asked, looking up at her and breaking our embrace.

"No. At least I don't think so. But there is so much hatred, so much anger. People want revenge on the Germans because of all they've lost. But what good is revenge? You become like your enemy. . ." Her voice trailed off, as if she had more to say but felt the futility of saying it.

"Killing a dog doesn't solve anything," I urged, feeling

my mother wavering. "Think of all the ways she can help us. She can guard us and let us know when people are coming. She can pull Rina's sled in the winter! I bet I could teach her to hunt; she probably knows how already."

"Mikhail, Mikhail," she said softly. "If we keep this dog, you must teach it not to bark. You must keep her out of sight. No one must know we have her." My mother looked at Zasha, who lifted her head and returned my mother's gaze. Her face softened. "She is beautiful."

"Why do we have to keep her a secret if it's not illegal?" I asked, knowing the answer.

She looked at me sharply. "Mikhail, we've been in a war for four years. Don't make me think I've raised my son to be stupid. If we keep this dog, she is kept out of sight. I don't want any more killing or dying. You know there are Russians who think it's their duty to destroy anything German."

"How can you say a dog has a nationality? Maybe she wasn't even born in Germany. Maybe she was born in Russia! Maybe she's a Russian shepherd."

"And maybe you should study law with your fancy arguments. Now go and wake Nikolai and Rina. We'll say prayers for this poor man and get him ready to take to the officials in the village."

"Yes, Mama. Thank you."

She shook her head as she left, as though wondering how she had let her heart get the better of her head. I turned to look one last time at the man with his dog. "Zasha – come!" She put her paw on Petr's arm and laid her head down so that she was turned away from me, as if she didn't want to hear, didn't want to know. I waited for a full minute, understanding that she was saying goodbye. Finally, I said again softly, "Zasha – come." With one last loving look at Petr, she jumped off the bed and followed me as I went to awaken my brother and sister.

That is how Zasha came to us, and why the two men in their stinking yellow van came to our house looking for her. It is why I created a hiding place for her at the furthest end of our farm. But it was only the beginning of our adventure.

CHAPTER THREE

Later that morning, after my mother bathed Petr and we all said our prayers for him, we loaded him – with some difficulty – into our hay cart. Paku pulled us into the village almost fifteen kilometres away.

Normally, we would talk and laugh and sing and tell jokes, but not on that day. It wasn't just that there was a dead man in our cart; it was also the problem of Zasha.

We had no choice but to leave her alone at the farmhouse. If anyone came to visit while we were gone, they would know about her. There was also the possibility she would escape. The doors were locked, of course, but as I told my mother, "If she were desperate, she could jump through a window!"

"Stop being so dramatic, Mikhail," she chided me. "If she's as clever as you think she is, she'll stay put and keep quiet." Still, I turned around several times before we reached our destination to see if she was following us. We passed our school at the ten-kilometre point. It housed all the children in the area in two wide rooms. I was grateful that there would be no more school until late in September.

Our village of Vasily was small, but we proudly called it a town, and it served the needs of the people well for sixty kilometres in any direction. Besides a post office, there was a bank, a dry goods, a hardware store, a grocer, a small court house and a blacksmith who did repairs on horseshoes. We even had a village newspaper that came out every week called the *Vasily Reporter*. At the end of the main street (and there were only two other streets) stood a small police station.

It was a busy Monday morning, with ten or so people going about their business. We saw a truck, other horse carts and even a small blue car. Nikolai and I observed it with interest.

"Children, come with me," my mother said as we pulled to a stop in front of the police station. The three of us glanced at one another as if to say, *Ten horses couldn't make us stay out here with a dead man while you have all the excitement of a police station*.

Nikolai held the battered wooden door open, and we entered. Because our class had visited the police station at least twice, it was familiar, and I was glad to see the same grey-haired police captain I'd seen before at his high desk.

"How may I help you?" he asked my mother with a warm smile.

"My son found an injured stranger near our house yesterday. The man had a bad infection and fever. During the night, he died."

"I see," he said, the smile fading, replaced by a more serious look. He took out a large pad of paper and picked up a pen. "Let's start at the beginning. Where was he found? Do you know his—" He interrupted himself to ask what he must have considered the most important question. "Where is this man now?"

"He is in our cart. In front of here," my mother answered, pointing in the direction of the street.

He handed my mother the paper and pen. "While I make arrangements for the body, would you please write down everything you remember about this man and as many details as possible." My mother nodded and settled herself on a bench along the wall to the right.

The captain called out to someone in the back of the station in an area we couldn't see. A stout young man with a thick neck appeared in a too-tight police uniform.

"We have a body, Ivan, brought to us by these kind people. Would you and Lev go and get him, please?"

"Lev isn't here, sir. He went to see about Mrs Leonid's cow." The captain shook his head slightly, as if to say concerns as small as someone's cow were starting to make him irritable.

"Boys," he said, addressing Nikolai and me, "can you help this officer bring the body into the station?"

"Yes, sir," we answered in unison. It was exciting to think we could be of help to grown policemen. Maybe we would even be able to go in the back, where neither of us had been before.

We followed Ivan, who stopped to hold the door open for a woman and a girl to enter. I was so excited about my duties, I hardly noticed them until I heard, "Mikhail and Nikolai Tarkov! What are you doing here?"

"Oh, Katia, hello," I said, recognizing my classmate. Nikolai and Rina greeted her, also.

I didn't dislike Katia, but I didn't like her, either. Nikolai and I discussed her once, and I think he said it best: "I always feel guilty when she looks at me, as if I've done something wrong."

"Yes," I had agreed, "and you feel as if she looks down on you."

Even though I hadn't asked her and wanted more than anything to be out with Ivan and poor Petr, she said, "I'm here as a reporter" – she shook a red clothbound notebook in her hand – "to see what's going on in the town. My father is the editor of the newspaper—"

"We know, Katia," my brother said. It was a fact she managed to include in almost every conversation.

"—and when I'm older I'll have a job like Miss Irina's. She's the reporter now." She paused and looked up at the young woman who accompanied her. "Maybe I'll even have her job!" she added with a laugh. Irina's close-lipped smile said it all. I think if she could have locked Katia in a cell, she would have.

"That's wonderful," I said, turning away from her. "Come on, Nikolai." We squeezed past them and ran out to the hay cart. Ivan had already unlatched the back and begun to pull Petr towards him by the legs.

"One of you get on each side," Ivan said. "Grab his back and shoulders when I pull him out." We did as Ivan asked; I almost lost my balance because the body was so heavy. It was also stiff, and, though I don't like to admit it, it was scary touching a dead person. Maybe Nikolai and Ivan felt the same way, because we carried him up the stairs and into the station in a matter of seconds.

"Where do you want him, Captain?" Ivan asked, breathing heavily.

The captain didn't have an immediate answer; the body seemed heavier and heavier with each passing moment.

"Both cells are occupied," he said finally, "and I don't want him on the floor. . . Put him on the table over there." He pointed to a table in the back corner of the room. We shuffled over there with Petr, and with much relief laid him on the long oak slab.

When I turned around, I bumped into Katia. "May I see?" she asked, making no effort to wait for an answer. She squinted her eyes as she brought her face close to Petr's face. "How old do you think he is?"

"It doesn't matter," I told her.

"Well, of course it does," she corrected me. "How will I ever write about his death unless I know all about him?"

"It's not your business," Nikolai said.

Katia stopped and looked at him directly. "Nikolai Tarkov, a dead man in the village is everyone's business. Unless you have something to hide." Nikolai uttered a sound of impatience and disgust, turned his back on her, and walked towards the captain and our mother.

Katia opened the red cloth notebook. "How did it happen? Did you find him? When did he die? And what is his name?"

Irina, who had been talking to Ivan, joined us. I didn't answer Katia's questions but stood staring at her, wondering how she could be so insensitive. She stamped her foot. "Mikhail! I asked you several questions. Answer me!"

"You're the one who wants to be a reporter. You'll

have to do the work yourself." I walked away from her and a giggling Irina.

My family gathered to leave a few minutes later, when my mother finished her written statement. While I held the door open for everyone, I overheard Irina giving Katia advice. "Haven't you ever heard the saying that you catch more flies with honey than with vinegar?"

"I know," she answered, "but my father says even horses benefit from the touch of a whip now and then." I assumed the frustrated sigh I heard as the door closed behind me was from Irina.

CHAPTER FOUR

As we left the main road going east and turned on to the gravel road of our farm, my heart beat faster. Nikolai was driving the cart. He stopped in front of our farmhouse to let Rina, me and my mother off before proceeding to the barn. Normally, I would help Nikolai unharness Paku, make sure he was fed and warm and put the cart back in its place. But on the way home, we had decided I should go in to see Zasha immediately.

I ran up the stairs ahead of Rina and my mother, dropping the key to the door in my efforts to unlock it quickly. Zasha was waiting three metres in front of the door. "Zasha!" I cried, and ran to kneel beside her, hugging her around the neck. She whimpered softly and nuzzled me back; I might even have felt the lick of her tongue on my ear. Rina came to join us.

"I'm not afraid of her," she said.

"Why should you be?"

"Because of what they do."

I frowned. "Like what?"

"Well," she said, adjusting herself on the floor next to me, "I heard the Germans taught them how to snatch babies from their carriages. Right in front of their mothers!"

"That's ridiculous," I said, stroking Zasha's head. "Can you imagine Zasha doing such a thing?"

"No, but I can imagine the Germans doing such a thing," she answered, a petulant look on her face. "They killed Papa, didn't they?"

"Don't say that! Don't ever say that!" I yelled in a voice so loud that Zasha flinched and stared at me with her ears pinned back. "You don't know he's dead."

"Children!" My mother came out of the kitchen walking fast, the heels of her shoes hitting hard on the wooden floor. "What now?"

"Rina said Zasha's a baby thief and—"

"I did not!"

"—and that the Germans killed Papa!" I was breathing heavily, and I knew I would cry in another minute if I wasn't careful.

My mother sat down with us on the floor in front of Zasha. She petted her head and smiled a little. "She really is beautiful, isn't she? I can't remember the last time I touched a dog." I felt the lump in my throat fade away.

"Probably Belka," I mused, thinking of our last dog, who tried harder than any two men to do her best at whatever task we gave her. She'd died of old age at least five years ago.

"Let me ask you a question." My mother paused as if gathering her thoughts. "Do you think the Russians are the heroes of this war?"

"Yes, Mama, yes!" Rina cried, clapping her hands together.

"And you?" she asked, looking at me.

"We won the war, so yes, I suppose we are heroes."

"Let me explain something, children. People sometimes do heroic things in a war, but everyone does terrible things. No one is only good, or only bad."

"That's not true," I said, not understanding what she meant.

"You want an example, of course." I wasn't sure I did, but she continued. "Do you know what we Russians did with dogs to help us fight?"

"No," I said, changing to a more comfortable position to hear what I was sure were going to be heroic dog stories.

"Well, first we starved the dogs. Then we put food under tanks and trained them to run under the tanks when they saw them to get the food. Next we strapped explosives on the backs of our starving dogs and let them loose on the battlefields to run under German tanks and blow them up."

"But Mama," Rina asked, looking confused and upset, "why did we do that?"

"To kill our enemies."

"But what about the poor dogs?"

"They died, of course." I stared at my mother, wishing she had not told me this awful story.

"And the Americans – do you think they are heroes?"

"Yes," I said, fearful of what she would say next.

"They used flamethrowers against their fellow human beings. Think about that. A machine that hurls fire at everything in its path."

"They were attacked. Shouldn't they fight back?"

"Yes, of course. Russia was attacked, too; we fought back very hard. What I'm saying is, people do terrible things in times of war. We did, too. Flamethrowers are now quite common in almost every army. No one's hands are clean." Now it was my mother who looked as if she might cry.

"But what about Papa?" Rina asked, drawing near to my mother and putting her head in her lap. "Do you forgive the Germans for that?"

My mother didn't answer. Zasha lay down, and she, too, put her head in my mother's lap. "Look – she likes you!" Rina said. My mother seemed surprised but pleased, and stroked Zasha's head and scratched her behind the ears.

Very softly I said, "There is always a chance he didn't. . ."

The front door opened quickly, and in came Nikolai.

"The very picture of family happiness! But shouldn't we lock the door if we want to keep Zasha a secret?"

My mother got up with one last pat on Zasha's head. "He's right. As of today, the door is locked even when we're home."

"We'd better keep a key hidden outside in case of emergency."

"Good idea, Mikhail," my mother said. "Always thinking ahead. You are very much like your father."

"But I look more like him," Nikolai said proudly.

"And I. . ." Rina began, and faltered. "I'm starting to forget what he looked like."

CHAPTER FIVE

During the last four years, since Germany invaded Russia, life had changed. My father's absence was the biggest change, of course, but it was also the first time I asked my mother for a certain food and was told there simply wasn't any.

"No strawberry jam?" I replied in disbelief when she said we'd eaten the last of it.

She shook her head. "I had to donate a portion of all our canned goods to the state fund. And you've seen people sneaking into our garden at night to steal our strawberries."

"Yes, and whatever else they could get," Nikolai added with a laugh. He kept a pitchfork near the back door and used it to run after them. The very sight of him and his weapon made the thieves run. All of us knew he'd never use it except to scare them, but we enjoyed watching the chase.

I studied my bare piece of brown bread. "Why should someone else have our jam and we don't?"

"Why should *we* have it and *they* don't? There is no answer for you except that we have to make do with what we've got." I remember my mother leaving the room after telling me this; I followed her a moment later. She stood outside at the top of the back steps, breathing heavily, and talking out loud as if she were having a conversation with someone. I guessed it was my father, because I'm almost sure she said, "Oh, Constantin!" just before she noticed me.

That is why having Zasha in our home that first night after Petr died was so thrilling; each of us seemed to be just a little bit more alive. It was as if Father Christmas had arrived six months late, with only one gift to be shared by four people, but it was the best, most magical present ever received, and got better and better the more it was played with. But sharing is rarely easy.

I assumed Zasha would sleep next to me in the room I shared with Nikolai. When the sound of Rina and my mother's talking and laughter floated all the way downstairs after supper, something told me I should investigate.

"What are you doing?" I asked, pushing open the door to Rina's room. She and my mother sat on the floor next to Rina's bed. Between them was a collection of ragged towels and an old blanket or two.

"Nothing," Rina answered, moving as though to block me from viewing their creation. I came in to see for myself, sitting on the end of Rina's bed.

"That looks like a giant pillow," I teased. "Is it for the monsters under your bed?" Rina glanced quickly at my mother and said nothing.

An awkward silence built up, making me nervous and suspicious. Just as I was about to demand that they tell me their secret, my mother said, "We were thinking it might be nice if Zasha slept in Rina's room." I was on my feet before she finished her sentence.

"No! I found Zasha! She's mine. She will sleep next to me in my room." My cheeks burned. If Zasha had been there, I would have picked her up and carried her out with me.

"She's yours?" my mother asked calmly.

"Yes," I insisted, outraged that Rina would think for even a moment that Zasha was her dog. My mother nodded as Rina's lower lip pushed out further and further, the way it did when she held back her tears.

"I'm the youngest." Rina's voice quavered. "If she slept with me, I would never be afraid at night."

"You're afraid of monsters that don't exist. Nikolai and I are in the room next to you if something really happens."

"I get scared; I need Zasha." It was all I could do to keep myself from kicking the bed they were making into a heap. Nikolai's steps echoed in the hall. He entered before I could respond.

"Look!" he said proudly. "I made a new collar for Zasha." He held up a two-centimetre-wide strip of leather that he had cleverly plaited. "I'm not sure yet how I'm going to fasten it. . . What's going on?" Zasha had followed him and stood next to him, ears up, an alert expression on her face.

My mother sighed and got up off the floor. "All right," she said in the tone that meant, *We have business to settle.* "Children. We are a family, are we not?"

"Yes, Mama," we all agreed.

"And what do families do?" I was still upset enough about Rina trying to claim Zasha that I didn't answer in case my answer worked in her favour. Nikolai saved me by stating our family motto.

"All for one, and one for all. Like the Three Musketeers!" His good nature shone from his face, even in that tense moment.

"That's right," my mother said. "If the presence of this dog in our lives causes unhappiness between us, she cannot stay."

"No!" I cried.

"Mother, what do you mean?" Nikolai asked, looking surprised and confused.

"She can sleep in Mikhail's room, Mama. I'm sorry." Rina jumped to her feet.

Even my mother's lips trembled in the way they did

when she struggled with her emotions. “Here’s what we’re going to do. Mikhail will feed Zasha and give her water. Nikolai, I want you and Mikhail to share grooming duties and run with her before dawn or after dark. Rina, I apologize, but Zasha will be sleeping in Mikhail’s room. But” – Rina’s desperate expression made Mother reach out and caress her hair “you and I will teach her how to act in the house. I think this bed we’re making might work just as well next to the fireplace in the kitchen, don’t you?” Rina nodded and took her hand.

“We’ll teach her how to shake hands, won’t we, Mama?” she said, calming down.

“Yes. Now, are we finished here? Is there anything else anyone wants to say?”

“Thank you, Mama,” Rina said. Nikolai, too, murmured his thanks.

“Yes,” I said. “Is Zasha my dog?” My mother gazed at me for what seemed like a long time.

“Are you my son?”

“Yes.”

“And yet you are your own person, are you not?”

“Yes.”

“You have your own thoughts and desires. Secrets, too, probably.”

“Well, I. . .”

"Zasha cannot be owned by you or us, any more than I own you children. But if we love her, she will become part of our family."

"Mother," I said, "with respect – you have not answered my question." I could feel Rina's and Nikolai's questioning looks at both me and my mother, but I continued to stare directly into my mother's eyes until she spoke.

She nodded her head slowly. "It's just like your father used to say."

"What, Mama, what did he say?" Nikolai asked, always anxious for any detail about him.

"Every group needs a leader."

"How did he . . . oh, yes." Nikolai lowered his voice as much as possible to imitate our father. "Whether you're in a company of soldiers, or digging potatoes, or playing in an orchestra, every group needs a leader." The happiness of the shared memory of our father broke the tension, and I relaxed for the first time since I'd entered Rina's room.

"We're going to let Zasha answer your question, Mikhail," my mother said. "All of you, out. Wait at the bottom of the stairs. Not you, Zasha." She took firm hold of Zasha's collar. Zasha pulled towards us children as we made our way reluctantly to the door.

"Then what?" Nikolai asked.

"One by one you are going to call Zasha to come to

you. You may call her name, and you may say 'come' or 'here', but nothing else. Two words only. Whoever Zasha comes to is her leader."

I didn't like this idea at all. "What if she's been taught to go to anyone who calls her name?" I said, my voice tight with fear that I would lose this game.

"You'll each get your turn. If she comes to all three of you, you will share her equally."

"And if she comes to just one of us?"

"Zasha has chosen that person to be her leader. That person gets to make the most important decisions about her."

Rina was already running down the hall towards the top of the stairs, her shoes slapping on the dark, worn wood. "I'm going to win!"

I turned my head for one last look at Zasha, who moved subtly, so ready to be going with us. "Don't say anything more to Zasha until you're down the stairs," my mother warned.

"Yes, Mama," I said, following my brother to join our sister for this awful game. How was I going to win? Nikolai's voice was deeper than mine and more commanding. Zasha seemed like she had a soft heart; she might go to Rina when she called just to make a little girl happy. And me, what did I have, I asked myself, watching each step under my feet. *Nothing*, I thought, *nothing at all*. Except . . . except that I found Zasha and Petr. It was *me* who said I would help him instead of running away when I saw the bleeding man. I was the one who called to her when Petr lay dead and she didn't want to leave him, and she followed.

"I will go last," I announced as I reached the ground floor.

Rina jumped up and down in place. "I'm first, I'm first!"

The three of us stood at the bottom of the staircase, looking up: Rina on the left, Nikolai next to her, and me on the right.

"Are you ready?" my mother called from Rina's room, her voice sounding muffled and far away.

"Yes," we answered.

"Count to five, and then one of you call her. And remember the rules!"

"One," Rina whispered, "two, three, four, five." Then, in a strong, loud voice, she cried, "Zasha – come to me!"

Nikolai turned to her and poked her arm with his elbow. "You used too many words! That's against the rules."

"Shhh," she said, her focus on the landing at the top of the stairs. My palms felt sweaty, my forehead tight, like it was made of metal. We waited at least thirty seconds. "Zasha, please come!"

"You're cheating," Nikolai told her. Still, no Zasha. I peered around Nikolai to see Rina. Her expression said she knew Zasha wasn't coming but didn't want to admit it.

Nikolai smiled as my mother called, "Next!"

In a calm, melodious voice, he counted to five. Then, with the authority of an officer, he called loudly, "Zasha, come here!"

"Mother said you could use only two words – you used three." He ignored me, waiting expectantly, standing tall, his posture erect.

Zasha never came. Nikolai was clearly disappointed and almost looked angry when he said to me, "If she doesn't come to you, she belongs to all of us equally."

"I know."

"All right, Mikhail, it's your turn," my mother said at last. I felt like I did when I walked on the rope we tied between two trees: focused, calm, excited.

"Zasha – come!" I called. I heard the tapping immediately, the sound of her hard nails upon the wood floor. In seconds she was at the second-floor landing, then rushing down the stairs towards me. I bent down on one knee and opened my arms. She tumbled into me, knocking me over, licking my face, making me laugh. Finally, I sat up.

Nikolai and Rina watched us, each of them with resignation in their eyes.

"Zasha told me she's hungry," I said, not wanting them to feel bad. "Would you two help me feed her? Maybe brush her hair a little?"

Rina's eyes widened. "Yes! And I could share my brush with her."

"I don't think so, my dear," my mother said, coming slowly down the stairs. "We'll find her something of her own. So . . . it's settled, then?"

Nikolai nodded. "It's all right," he said stoically. "She will be part of our family, like you said. But someone must be her leader, and she has chosen Mikhail." My hand never left her thick, soft fur; I stroked her from head to tail several times.

"I'm going out to the barn, Mama," Rina cried as she ran towards the back door. "Maybe Paku has an old brush."

"Do you remember what your father used to say, Mikhail?"

"What, Mama?"

"To whom much is given, much is expected." I smiled and stood up. "And do you remember what I said?"

I nodded. "No one must know of this dog. No one."

CHAPTER SIX

The next week was a time of intense training for Zasha. We all did our parts, but it was settled that Zasha looked to me as her new master.

I taught her verbal commands – *stay*, *go*, *no*, *yes*, *run*, *wait*, *come*, *down* and others. She seemed to know most of them already, and those she didn't know she learned quickly.

Rina invented her own game with Zasha. She'd say, "Zasha, kitchen!" and teach her to go to that room and wait. "Zasha, back room! Zasha, front room! Zasha, door!" It was very helpful, especially because Nikolai taught her how to fetch things like shoes, books and jackets. By the end of the first week, I could say, "Zasha, upstairs. Shoes. Come here," and she'd run upstairs, grab the shoes in her mouth and bring them to me wherever I was.

Now that it was not quite as difficult to get food and supplies as it had been during the worst of the war, my mother was happy to make Zasha little round treats of cornmeal and molasses. Zasha didn't need bribing to perform the tasks we requested of her, but she was always excited to receive a treat as a reward for doing them.

We guessed that Zasha weighed thirty kilograms. A dog that size needs lots of exercise, and running from room to room wasn't going to give her what she needed. Nikolai and I took turns each morning before dawn walking and running with her down one of the three paths that led to the forest. It was harder on us than it was on her because Vasily is located far north. In June, our days are long and our nights brief. We had to get up very early to walk her and get back home before dawn, and stay up very late to walk her after dark. It was an imperfect arrangement, but none of us wanted to risk letting the outside world know about Zasha unless we could be sure it was safe.

An uninvited visitor made it clear we would have to change something.

Zasha heard the approach before any of us one morning, just as we were finishing our breakfast of tea and bread. She stood up abruptly next to the kitchen table and stared hard at the door that led to the hall and the front door. She growled softly.

"Someone's coming!" I cried. "Is the door locked?"

"I think so," my mother said, getting up and rushing to the door. It was locked.

"Where shall we put her?" Nikolai whispered as my mother came back into the kitchen.

"Upstairs," Rina said, "in my room."

"Good idea," my mother agreed. "I'll close the door to the stairway." Like most houses built where the winters are severe, the family bedrooms were upstairs. When the cold came we would close off the stairway, keeping all the warm air up there at night.

As Rina ran off with Zasha, the first knock came. "I'll answer it," I said, waiting a few moments to make sure Rina and Zasha were settled upstairs.

"Help me with the dishes, Nikolai," my mother said. "Act as normal as possible."

I opened our sturdy front door and was surprised and not at all happy to see Katia Klukova; a small basket hung from the crook of her arm.

"Mikhail Tarkov!" she said brightly. "Beautiful weather we're having. May I come in?" She passed by me and into the house.

"Why are you here?" I blurted out.

"That's not a very nice welcome," she reprimanded me. "You should offer me tea."

"We just finished our morning tea. I suppose I could ask my mother to make more." She smiled her consent and looked around our entranceway, with its doors, stairs and halls that let you go in four different directions in the house.

"Hello, Katia," my mother said, coming out of the kitchen as she dried her hands on a dish towel. "How is your family?"

"Fine, Mrs Tarkov. I hope you don't mind, but I've come to visit Rina." Katia had never come before to play with Rina. In fact, she was closer to my age of thirteen than to Rina's age of nine.

"Rina's not feeling well today, Katia. But I am sure she will be happy you stopped by." I was impressed by the ease with which my mother handled the situation.

Katia looked displeased. "I'm so sorry to hear that. Mrs Stolypin at the dry goods store told me you and Rina were there recently buying cloth for a new dress. I brought some ribbons for Rina that I thought might go well with it." She reached in her basket and pulled out blue, pink and lavender strands of ribbon and handed them to my mother.

"What a very generous thought, Katia," my mother said, accepting them. "It's so nice to be able to buy things like ribbons and buttons again, isn't it?" I could see she was annoyed that Mrs Stolypin was discussing her purchases, although I don't think Katia noticed. Nikolai leaned against the doorway to the kitchen, listening.

"May I stay for a while, Mrs Tarkov? I would love to hear all about that poor man who died."

The expression on my mother's face remained calm and assured as she said, "There's nothing to tell. Mikhail found him, he collapsed, his arm was terribly infected, and he died." Turning to me, she added, "Mikhail, you were going to chop some firewood for me this morning. Perhaps Katia would like to help you?" It was clear she wanted Katia out of the house.

"Yes," I said, hiding my smile. "I could use your help, Katia."

"I'm not dressed for farm work, but . . . do you have any animals I could meet?" I stole a glance at my mother, waiting for a cue from her. All I wanted was for Katia to go away.

"We have an old horse," my mother said with a laugh. "Some geese and chickens. Nothing exceptional. Why don't we go out to the barn and I'll show you?"

Katia smiled broadly. "I love animals," she said, following my mother down the front stairs like a baby duck follows her mama.

"Stay with Rina," I whispered to Nikolai before I left. He nodded his consent, carefully opened the door to the stairwell and disappeared.

The gravel crunched under our feet as we made our

way to the barn. "I don't have brothers or sisters," I heard Katia tell my mother as I ran to catch up with them. "Maybe that's why I love animals so much." After a brief pause, in a funny voice that told me she'd been waiting to say it, Katia added, "And speaking of animals, I stayed at the police station for a long time after you left the other day, and guess what?"

"I can't imagine," my mother murmured.

"That man's clothes were not just dirty – they had hairs all over them."

"Oh," my mother responded pleasantly, pulling open the wide barn door. "How interesting. I certainly hope the police can locate his family. Now, Mikhail, where is the wood we talked about?"

"I think they were *dog* hairs."

"Dog hairs?" my mother said in a sceptical tone. "I don't see how that could be possible. All the dogs have disappeared since the war started."

"I think he had a dog with him. I'm almost sure of it." She said it in a funny, defiant way, as if daring us to deny it. And then, as she spotted the mother goose and her goslings, she exclaimed, "Oh! That's the cutest thing I've ever seen!" She looked at my mother and me as if we, too, should find this common sight extraordinary.

"Your family doesn't keep animals, Katia?" my mother

asked. Katia shook her head as she knelt down next to the goose pen.

"No, just a horse. My father doesn't know how to farm, and my mother, well, she doesn't like things like this. What are their names?" She looked up at me.

"Whose names?"

"The mama and her babies."

"They don't have names. They're geese." Farm children know better than to name animals that will be sold or eaten; we don't want to become too attached.

"Mikhail Tarkov, how could you be so negligent? Well, if you can't be bothered to name them, I'll do it myself. You don't mind, do you, Mrs Tarkov?" She didn't wait for an answer before continuing. "Let's see. . . Mama, your name is Sunshine. And babies, you are . . . Sunflower, Daisy and Sweetpea!" Katia looked proud and happy after she'd named the animals and reached into the pen to pet one of the baby geese.

"If you do that, the mama goose will bite your fingers!" I warned her. I was amazed she'd had the nerve to name our animals and wouldn't have been all that sorry if the mama goose – excuse me, *Sunshine* – had got to Katia's fingers before she could pull them away. But she stood up immediately, holding her basket behind her even as the mama began to flap her wings and move towards us.

"There's our horse" – I pointed across the barn to where Paku stood – "and he has a name, thank you." I hoped she'd get the hint that it was time for her to be going. Instead, she stood still, hands on her hips, looking around curiously.

"Katia, dear, I'm so sorry, but the boys really must get started on their work for the day, especially because they will have to do Rina's as well." My mother left the barn, forcing the reluctant Katia to follow. "How did you get here? You didn't walk all the way from town, did you?" I followed a few steps behind them, listening.

"No, Mrs Tarkov. I rode to your neighbours' house on my horse. I needed to speak with them to see if they knew anything about the man who died. Or about the dog."

"Where is your horse now?"

"I left it there so I could walk here." *So you could spy on us*, I thought, *and sneak up and take us by surprise*.

"Mikhail," my mother called back to me, "why don't you start on the firewood while I walk Katia to the road?"

"Yes, Mother." When she returned, we waited for five minutes out in front to make sure Katia wasn't coming back.

"Lock the door," my mother said as we rushed into the house; I needed no reminding. My mother opened the door to the stairway and called for Rina, Nikolai and Zasha. They came running.

"We watched you from the window," Rina said. "What did she want?"

"To visit you," I said almost angrily.

"Me? We never play together. She ignores me at school."

"And she gave our geese names!"

"She did? What are they?" I would rather have walked sixty kilometres barefoot than answer Rina's question.

"She knows she's on the trail of something," Nikolai said. "We haven't seen the last of her."

"Zasha, upstairs!" I said, shaken by Katia's visit. I followed Zasha into the safety of the room I shared with Nikolai and we lay down on the bed together. Within a few seconds, Nikolai came and sat at the foot of the bed and Rina lay down on Zasha's other side.

"Where do you think Zasha came from?" Nikolai asked as he stroked the thick black and beige fur near her tail.

"I've been asking myself the same question," I said, scratching behind her ears.

"I think she belonged to a king!" Rina put her arms around Zasha's neck and hugged her. "Who else would have such a beautiful dog? And you can see that she loves children. Maybe the king had many children!"

"There are no kings. Even the tsar is gone," Nikolai

scoffed. "But if she did belong to a king, his children were definitely boys. You can tell by the intelligent look in her eyes. They must have taught her to hunt and track and guard."

"They were girl children," Rina insisted. "If they weren't, Zasha wouldn't be so playful and let you love her so much."

I rolled on my back, my fingers still slipping through Zasha's silky fur. "I think . . . Zasha is a magical creature, like a griffin or a dragon. If we don't treat her well, she will fly back to the land she came from and leave us alone again."

"Don't go, Zasha!" Rina said, hugging her even tighter.

"She doesn't need to worry about her treatment here," Nikolai said emphatically. "That means she can stay for ever."

"Zasha," I said softly, not caring if Nikolai or Rina laughed at me, "I will never leave you. Do you understand? Never! I will die before I let anyone hurt you. And I will keep Katia Klukova far, *far* away." My last statement made my brother and sister laugh, but Zasha nuzzled closer to me. She must have known how serious I was about working out a way to keep my promise.

CHAPTER SEVEN

To those who are used to cities, the countryside looks like an empty place, peppered with isolated farmhouses and barns. If you live in the countryside, you know how active it is. You may wake to find a beggar at your back door, offering to sharpen your knives in exchange for a good meal. Woodsmen traverse the boundless forests in all seasons, half hermits, half madmen. Neighbours visit, sharing stories and local gossip.

With all of this in mind, Nikolai and I still came to the conclusion that we had to find somewhere outdoors, away from the house, where we could hide Zasha if necessary. We stood under an old beech tree discussing the possibilities. Zasha lay on her side next to us in the thick, cool shade. We were only a hundred metres off one of the paths to the forest, tucked down and away behind a small rocky hill, next to a trickle of a stream.

Nikolai pointed to a small opening near the base of the hill, not big enough to be called a cave, but large enough for a small boy to crawl into on his hands and knees, as we had done many times. "I think if we were very careful, we could hollow that opening out just a little more. Maybe even put sticks in there to act like supports."

I'd got stuck inside it once and had no desire to go in again. "Don't you think the earth would collapse if we dug more out?"

"All we need to do is make it big enough for Zasha to walk into, turn around and lie down. That won't be much. Plus room for the supports, like I said."

I nodded, thinking he could be right. "If we gathered rocks, we could arrange them a metre in front of the cave opening and make it look natural, but leave a space on the side so Zasha could come and go."

"Yes!" He got up and pointed to the stream. "And she'll always have fresh water. It's low now, but it never dries up."

"What if someone sees her?"

"There is danger for her no matter where we keep her. The workers won't be back till September. Even then, they work so hard all day that the last thing they want to do is explore the land."

"Will we have to keep her hidden for ever?" I asked, thinking how I longed to run with her through the fields.

"I don't know. But for now, yes. Until everyone stops being so mad at Germany."

"Do you . . . do you think that will ever happen?"

"For some, no. But so many dogs starved and disappeared during the war that I think people will soon start looking for dogs again. Maybe they will forget their hatred, and if they meet a beautiful German shepherd, they'll admire her, not want to destroy her."

"I don't think there are any more German shepherds in Russia," I said, sitting down next to Zasha and stroking her neck.

"Maybe in some of the cities," Nikolai suggested half-heartedly.

"I don't think so. The battles were too destructive, too long. The siege of Leningrad lasted two and a half years! I think they've either been killed or starved or taken by the army to blow up tanks, like Mother told us." Nikolai sat down heavily next to me, nodding his head. "She might be the last German shepherd in all of Russia."

"Russia's very big," Nikolai argued.

"I think they're all gone," I said, my voice soft with fear. "And I think if they find Zasha, they'll kill her, too."

"Who's 'they'?" he asked after a moment.

"Anyone who thinks a good Russian must hate even the dogs of their enemy."

"Mother said they aren't our enemy any more because they surrendered and the war is over."

"Our mother is kinder and more logical than most." I stood up nervously. "Come on, Nikolai. We need to find two more hiding places."

"Why? This one is perfect. It's a kilometre from the house, it has water. . ."

"I know, I know. It's just that we have to be prepared for the unexpected." He stared into the distance and pulled at the grass, concentrating. "There's the workers' shelter down at the southwest end of the farm," I said, referring to a square hut where the farmhands sheltered from heavy storms during the harvest.

Nikolai looked doubtful. "A building like that would be too obvious."

"Yes, but for an emergency it would do."

"What kind of an emergency?"

"Let's say the Gypsies made a camp here."

"They know better than to camp on farmland. I've heard that some were even beaten in the southern provinces for doing that."

"I still see them sometimes in the forest."

"All right, for an 'emergency' we'll use the workers' shelter. But you said we need three. . . I can't think of another place. The land is too flat."

"Our house."

"Don't be ridiculous."

"I'm serious. If we don't have time to hide Zasha out here, we have to have something ready – in the house, the barn, I don't know."

We were walking back and forth restlessly now. Zasha sat up, watching us intently. "We need to trick the eye," I said, thinking out loud. "A person sees something and makes an assumption. Like when you see someone in uniform, you automatically believe that person is what their uniform says they are."

"You're saying we need to find something like that at home, that someone will see, but overlook."

"The barn has possibilities," I continued, "but the building is so open. You could hide a small object there in the hay; it would be perfect. But I don't think it's our answer for Zasha."

"The cellar?" Nikolai asked in a tone that suggested he knew as he said it that it was a bad idea.

I shook my head. "Somewhere in Mother's room?"

"There is that L-shaped cupboard. . ."

"It will come to us when we're back home and looking hard. For now, let's dig out the little cave for Zasha. At least we'll have something ready."

Zasha trotted behind us with interest as we gathered rocks and sticks, and with the help of a few sharp ones, we began to create her hiding place. Nikolai did the digging, knowing my dislike of the small space. I layered rocks, mud from the streambed, and the plants that surrounded us into a little wall in front of the entrance to the cave, mimicking the hillside as well as I could.

After almost an hour of work we stopped, took off our shirts and sat at the edge of the creek, soaking our feet in the cool water; Zasha lay between us.

Without realizing it, I began to sing a song our grandmother used to sing to me. "*Shine, shine, my star. Shine, my twinkling star. You are my dearest one, there will be no other.*" By the time I got to the third line, Zasha emitted a sound halfway between a moan and a howl. She kept it up in the fourth line, a little louder.

Nikolai and I stared at each other in astonishment. Up until that moment, Zasha had not yet barked or made a sound louder than a growl.

"Sing the second verse," Nikolai demanded.

"*When the night comes down, a lot of stars shine in the sky. . .*" Zasha howled along. Her tones were long, her pitches varied.

"She's singing!" I cried, and continued the song. "*But you're the only one I see, shine, my little star.*"

Nikolai fell back on the ground, laughing. "I can't believe it! Zasha likes to sing!" He tried another song, one we'd learned at school. She repeated her performance, snout high in the air, her mouth a little askew as she felt for the notes she so obviously heard.

I lay down on my side on the soft earth, facing Nikolai and Zasha, my feet still touching the gently moving water. "I love her almost as much as I love Mama and Papa," I confessed.

"But more than Rina?" he joked.

"Equal to Rina . . . on one of her good days!"

Nikolai got up and stretched. "We should get back to work. I wonder what other songs she knows."

I petted Zasha's head. "I'll bet she happens to know every song we know."

Nikolai sang the first few notes of the national anthem. Zasha joined him. I hugged her and stood up. "Let's make a hiding place worthy of such a singer."

As I walked back towards the cave, I sang again: "*Shine, shine, my star. . .*" Zasha followed me, howling along. Nikolai sang, too. "*Shine, my twinkling star. You are my dearest one. There will be no other.*" Zasha looked at each one of us in turn when we'd finished, proud as any opera star, ready for her encore.

CHAPTER EIGHT

It was just days after we'd finished "the cave", as we now referred to Zasha's main hiding place, when the men in the yellow van showed up. Only luck saved us and Zasha. I'd awakened before dawn from a bad dream. In my dream, Katia was dressed in an army uniform. She came to our farm with lots of soldiers who spread out across the fields, beating the brush and the ground and the trees with sticks. "There it is! There it is!" Katia shouted again and again. I woke myself up trying to cry out for them to stop, succeeding only in emitting a strangled moan.

When I opened my eyes, Zasha was sitting up just centimetres from me, watching my solitary struggle. The dream felt more real than our room, where Nikolai lay sleeping soundly, unaware of the drama taking place in the bed across from him.

In the cold and the dark I dressed and ran with Zasha to the cave. We watched dawn break by the side of the creek – pink and blue and golden. Only hours after that, when I returned to the farm for food for us both, the men surprised my brother and me in the barn. And the day was only to get worse.

We'd rushed to the cave to make sure Zasha was safe after we felt certain the men were gone for good. She stood in front of the entrance, tail wagging, whimpering in excitement at our arrival.

"Zasha – cave!" I said, realizing I was going to have to teach her to stay inside the cave until I signalled her to come out. We ran to join her in the cramped space behind the wall we'd built, still shaken from our encounter.

"Oh, Zasha," Nikolai said with a sigh, "if you only knew. . ."

"Such a good girl," I murmured, caressing and petting her, feeding her the bits of bread and cheese I'd brought for her breakfast.

"Who do you think they were, Mikhail?" Nikolai asked.

I shook my head but answered, "Thieves. Who else would show us their guns like that? But where would they have heard a rumour about a German shepherd?"

"I think they heard it from Katia."

I was sceptical. "Katia and her family wouldn't associate with such men."

"Then perhaps from someone she spoke to. Don't you remember when she came to our house a week ago?"

"Of course I do." I poked at the dirt with a short stick.

"She'd been to the Golovin farm first to ask about Petr—"

"And the dog," I finished. "They could have mentioned it to someone who talked to someone else who. . ."

"Exactly. And what business is it of hers?" After a long silence, Nikolai looked around and, with a laugh, said, "Why are we still in the cave? Let's play with Zasha!" We scrambled from the tight space, stretching and breathing deeply of the fresh air.

In the previous few days, Nikolai and I had built an obstacle course made up mostly of bales of hay. We were teaching Zasha how to jump over, run around and go under all of the challenges we'd created for her.

"Nikolai! Watch what she learned yesterday! Zasha!" I said to get her attention. She waited, tense, ready to run alongside me. "Zasha – go!" She ran and leaped over the first bale of hay, then turned back and jumped over two stacked one upon the other. Then down into a small ditch I'd dug, which was covered by two more bales of hay; she was in and out in seconds.

"Fantastic!" Nikolai cried. "Let me try." She obeyed his commands and repeated her speedy and graceful performance.

"If we teach her all these things, Nikolai," I said,

breathing heavily after all the running back and forth I'd been doing with Zasha, "she's invaluable. No one would want to hurt her."

"Although they might still want to steal her."

"It's our job to make sure that never happens."

"Agreed," he said quickly, as though he wished he hadn't made reference to the men who'd scared us so badly that morning. "And she'd be a perfect hunting dog," he continued, tossing her one of the small treats my mother baked for her. "Now she can jump over all kinds of things. Maybe she could even help find lost people. Her sense of smell is amazing. She led me to a nest of rabbits yesterday, but she didn't touch one of them. She just wanted me to know they were there."

"You didn't tell me! Show me; I want to see them."

Nikolai pointed towards the path that led around the hill that shielded us. "They're down by that patch of currants Mother loves. . . Wait! Look at Zasha!"

I turned in fear to look at her, not knowing what he meant. She stood rigidly, ears up, leaning forward, tail tense and quivering, front paw up like a pointer. "Someone's coming," I whispered as loudly as I dared. "Zasha – cave!" Her head snapped around towards me, and she followed as I rushed to the entrance of our hiding place. "Zasha – stay!" I said as quietly and vehemently as possible after she'd gone in, turned around and laid down. Her intelligent brown eyes told me she understood.

I ran from the cave and leaped over a hay bale, as if this were my obstacle course, my playground. Nikolai understood immediately and dived into the little covered ditch. Coming out the other side, he said, "Still a little tight for me, Mikhail."

"Help me dig, then," I answered, playing along, anxiously awaiting the sound or sight of someone stumbling into our hidden area.

Nikolai and I turned as one when the faint sounds began to define themselves as *clip-clop*, *clip-clop*. Sauntering slowly into view was Katia Klukova astride a large brown mare. She seemed as surprised to see us as we were surprised to see her.

"Oh, Mikhail, Nikolai . . . I didn't expect to see you," she said, bringing the large horse to a stop.

"No?" I said, walking casually towards her. "But you're here at our farm." Nikolai, who was brushing the dirt off his clothes, came to join us, patting the mare on the neck.

"What are you looking for, Katia?" Nikolai asked bluntly.

"Nothing, really, I just. . ." She swung herself off the horse and on to the ground.

"What is all this?" she asked, motioning towards the obstacle course we'd set up.

"We're doing physical training," I said. "Nikolai may go into the army when he's old enough, and I might follow." Katia strolled around the small area, holding her mare by its reins.

"Let me see what you do," she demanded.

"Not unless you do it, too," Nikolai answered. She gave a small laugh and shrugged her shoulders.

"I don't think I want to ruin this dress for that."

"You never answered Nikolai's question," I said, anxious to have her gone. "Why are you here?"

"Actually, he asked me what I was looking for," she corrected me, then turned to study us both carefully before continuing. "I am looking for something, I just don't know what it is."

"That makes no sense," I said, jumping on top of one of the hay bales.

"Yes, it does. I mean, if you are a reporter like I am."

"You're not a reporter," Nikolai scoffed, as I smiled and tried not to laugh.

"My father is—"

"The editor of the newspaper," Nikolai and I said along with her.

"Stop it. He's assigned me to this very important story of the dead stranger."

"I thought that the actual reporter, Miss Irina, who

actually writes for the paper, who has actual training and an actual job with the paper, was writing the story."

"I am assisting her. That's why I'm here, searching out details that will help us solve this mystery."

"All you're doing is trespassing on our land."

"Is there something you don't want me to see, Mikhail Tarkov?" She walked up so close to me that I could smell the faint milky scent of her breath.

"You're just nosy," I said, making a run for another bale of hay, easily jumping over it.

"And unqualified," Nikolai added. "Where's Irina?"

"Searching documents somewhere," she said with a wave of her hand. "Not doing what she *should* be doing."

"Which is?"

"Finding out who killed that man."

"He died of an infection. Maybe you should spend more time 'searching documents somewhere' like Irina."

"Tell me what happened," she said, ignoring my comment.

"Our mother already gave the police a statement. Read it."

"I have, but it's not very informative. I have a theory of my own."

"I'll bet you do," Nikolai said, not bothering to hide his amusement.

"It's my belief he was a German spy."

Both Nikolai and I laughed out loud. "A spy? How did you come to that conclusion?"

"Stop laughing!" she cried, stamping her right foot.

"You're scaring the horse," I said. "And aren't you a little old to be stamping your feet?"

"I'm sorry, Snowflake," she cooed to her horse. "Did I scare you? Do you want a treat? Does Snowflake want a treat?" She reached in the pocket of her dress and pulled out the nub of a carrot. The horse licked it out of her open palm.

"Snowflake?" Nikolai said, suppressing a laugh. "She's a beautiful horse, but she's the colour of mud." I stared at Katia, marvelling that she could change from a hostile interrogator to a sweeter-than-honey girl who talked to her horse in a matter of seconds.

"As I was saying," she continued, sounding like her normal self, "I'm sure he was a spy, and he was found here on your land. If he was alive and you helped him, you could be traitors. Your whole family could be traitors."

I felt so angry at hearing her outrageous idea – more of an accusation – that I wanted to wrestle her to the ground, like I would have if a boy had said the same thing, and hold her down until she took it back. Nikolai saved me from my own temper.

"Oh, yes. He was a spy. He told us so. And he had a secret decoder machine in his pocket."

"And a magnifying glass and a telescope," I said, playing along.

"Mikhail, don't forget that he could hear transmissions from outer space through the buttons on his hat."

"He also told me he saw ghosts and talked to angels."

Katia looked agitated as she turned her horse around and walked him down the path the way she'd come in. "He had a dog," she said over her shoulder. "The police captain let me take some of the hairs from the man's coat. He thought they were from a horse. But I took them to a man who breeds dogs. They were long and light at the root and black at the tip. He said that meant they could very well be the hairs of a German shepherd."

"I don't believe you. What man?" I cried.

"Dimitri Moravsky. He's starting a kennel soon; well, as soon as he can get the right dogs."

"He is? Where? How did you meet him?"

"If you lived nearer to town, you'd have heard of him. Everyone is so excited. But what a strange man." I was simultaneously excited and frightened.

"How can he start a kennel if he doesn't have the right dogs?"

She shrugged, still looking intently at everything

around her. "He has connections with the Red Army. They're going to breed a dog, a special Russian dog, that will take the place of all the old types of guard dogs we used before."

Nikolai and I were walking closer to her, as though she had a magnetic field we were helplessly drawn to.

"What do you mean when you say he was strange?"

"He was easily agitated. I'm sure it was because he was a soldier." I decided not to antagonize her further by suggesting perhaps *she* was the cause of his agitation, and not the war.

"Where is this kennel?"

"Why do you want to know?" she asked suspiciously.

"You said 'everyone' knows. Why shouldn't we?" I picked up a pebble from the ground and hurled it casually against the hillside to hide my excitement from Katia.

She still seemed reluctant to share her information, but finally said, "Do you know the abandoned dairy farm to the north? About three kilometres from here?"

"Where the Orlovs used to live?"

She nodded, then said brusquely, "I have to go."

"Don't you want to ask us more questions?" Nikolai teased her.

"I'm not a fool, Nikolai Tarkov, and I'm certain you know much more than you're saying."

"Like what?"

"That. . ." Here she faltered. "That maybe the man wasn't alone. Or he told you something important before he died. Or he still had his dog with him. His German dog."

"He did tell us something," I agreed. "He told us the war is over."

"Hadn't you heard?" Nikolai asked. "It ended not too long ago. Thank goodness he told us, or we might be out looking for German soldiers in the trees right now."

Katia sniffed. "I don't care if you laugh. There's something strange about all this."

"Be sure and let us know!" I said, doing a cartwheel to show her how unconcerned I was.

"I think his dog is still around here, and I'm going to find it."

"And then what?" I laughed, pushing down every fearful feeling that bubbled up in me.

"Bring him to justice."

"What – a trial? Do you have a good dog translator?"

"Don't be stupid. He'll be treated like all other German shepherds: he'll be killed."

"What a noble goal – to kill an innocent animal." There was an edge in my voice now as I pictured Zasha and the harm that could befall her. "How can you pretend to love animals – and talk to your horse like he understands you – and even *think* of taking the life of a dog?"

"Those dogs were our enemies, too. The Germans trained them to hunt people and to kill."

"All armies did that with dogs. So did we."

When she reached the end of the path before it wound around the rocky outcropping, she glanced around once more before mounting her horse. As she gave it a kick in its sides with her heels, she said, "It's not only dogs that can sniff out what's hidden."

CHAPTER NINE

We huddled at the entrance to the cave for half an hour after Katia left before we felt safe enough to let Zasha out.

"We should go," Nikolai said finally.

"No. I'm staying here with Zasha till it's dark. Then we'll go home."

Nikolai looked doubtful. "That's a long time from now."

"I know."

"We promised Mother we'd clean the barn."

"How can we leave Zasha alone with Katia snooping around? She was only metres away from her hiding place!"

Nikolai stood, surveying the little area we'd hoped would be so safe and private. "I don't mind cleaning the barn, but I'm not doing the goose pen. The mama goose always bites me."

I laughed. "That's because she thinks you want to cook her for dinner!" He tried to laugh, too, but she had a mean bite and had outrun Nikolai more than once.

"I'll clean the goose pen tomorrow if you do the rest."

"Done. Now, empty your pockets."

I pulled out some string, two butterscotch sweets that had no wrappers, a few coins and a small compass that always pointed south.

"That's all? Didn't you bring any food for yourself?"

I shook my head. "I forgot with all the . . . excitement."

"Now that Zasha is with us, we have to be prepared."

"Prepared for what?"

"Prepared for anything." Nikolai produced two items from one of his pockets that made me feel envious: a roundish scrap of steel and a piece of flint, for starting a fire. "Here." He held them out to me. "You can't come home till dark, and you'll get cold. I think a small fire would be all right. There's plenty of tinder around. Just don't make it too big."

I nodded and looked at him gratefully. "You don't happen to have any food, do you?" He reached in his other pocket and handed me its contents.

"Two treats for Zasha. You'll have to wait till you get home to eat." It seemed an eternity away. "Practise with Zasha. It's the perfect opportunity, but keep an eye out." I waved as he left for the farmhouse, trying not to feel the pangs of hunger that pinched at my stomach.

I took Nikolai's advice and for the next two hours practised every trick I could think of with Zasha. We even played a form of hide-and-seek where I would tell her to stay, hide as far away from her as I could in thirty seconds, and then give a short whistle. She found me immediately every time, but seemed as exhilarated as I was by the new game.

I guessed it was late afternoon when we sat by the little creek and had long drinks of water. "Come on, Zasha," I said after a short rest. "Let's find some tinder for a fire." I easily collected a pile of twigs, bits of bark, dead or dry grasses, and even a broken branch the size of my forearm and piled them in front of the cave just inside the protective wall.

Zasha settled herself, watching me curiously as I hit the steel with the flint again and again. Finally, I saw a spark and leaned my head down quickly to blow it into an ember. A zip of red flashed down from a bit of grass and spread into a warm yellow flame.

The fire grew to the size of my fist. That's as big as I wanted it to get, but even that required tending and feeding. It smelled of home, of comfort, of goodness. Zasha moved a few centimetres closer to me and the fire, and rested her head comfortably on her paws.

My butterscotch sweets were long gone. I felt in my pocket for one of her two treats. "Here, girl." She looked at me and the little round biscuit in my hand, touched it lightly with her nose, and looked away. "Zasha, I know you're hungry. Here, girl." She looked again, blinked her eyes twice, and turned away.

"Oh. . ." I thought I understood. "Zasha." She looked at me as I took the tiniest bite from her treat. Then I laid it in my palm and offered it to her. It was gone in a lick and barely chewed before it was swallowed. "You're the best dog in the world," I told her, deeply touched that she wouldn't eat if there was nothing for me. "Here's another one." We went through the same ritual. I had to remember to tell my mother that the treats she made for Zasha tasted good. With some sugar and a few raisins, I'd eat ten.

I fanned the flame of the little fire, added bits of wood and bark, and lay down next to Zasha not too far from it. The fur at her neck tickled my nose. "Did you have a papa, Zasha?" I asked her. "Of course you did, what a silly question. What was he like?" I stroked the fur on her back slowly, gently. "Do you remember him? Was it he who taught you to be so smart and loving?" She lay quietly next to me as the fire warmed us. Little by little, the more I petted her, she rolled on her side so I could pet her stomach. Whenever I stopped, she reached out and pawed my arm twice, letting me know I was not to stop.

"Was there ever such a good girl as you?" I whispered, rubbing her tummy. She touched me again as I yawned and settled in closer to her. "Why don't you tell me about your brothers and sisters?" I pictured five or six little Zashas tumbling together, their ears still soft and floppy, their pink tongues out as they panted after play, furry round balls of fun. That was the image that captured my mind as I fell asleep.

CHAPTER TEN

It seemed like hours later when I was awakened by the rumble of her low growl. "What is it, girl?" It took me a minute to remember where I was. It was dark; the air was cold, and the fire long dead. I heard the faint sound of voices. Zasha sat up, tense and alert. "No," I whispered, putting my arm around her. "Stay here."

The voices got louder. They were boisterous; there were three or maybe four of them, it was hard to tell. Once they entered the semi-enclosed area where we'd set up Zasha's obstacle course, I could hear every word as the sound bounced around the rocky walls.

"Sergei, you idiot!" one exclaimed. There was laughter and the *thud* of something hitting the ground.

"Call me an idiot, but I'm not going a step further. We're camping here."

"That's because you're too drunk to go a step further!"

"No, no," he said, laughing. "I could walk all night if I had to."

"Well, you do have to," another one said. "We all promised we wouldn't stop until we reached Viktor's hometown." There was a rattle that sounded like someone unpacking cooking gear.

"I'm tired," the petulant Sergei responded.

"I've been stuck in the army for four years, and I'm not going to stop until I'm home." I assumed it was Viktor speaking. Then there was even louder clanging and crashing, as if someone fell, and more laughing.

"Neither of you can walk!"

"Which is the reason we should camp here."

The one who seemed like he wasn't drunk said, "A rest, then, that's all. I want to get home, too, and I have further to go."

"Poor Boris," the voice I now recognized as Viktor said. "Look what the army's done to him. He's sober, disciplined and dutiful."

"One hour, that's all," Boris answered. "No fire, no tents."

Cries of protest went up from the inebriated Viktor and Sergei. "You're worse than the army. We'll freeze! We'll starve! We'll. . ." Then I heard a giant belch and more laughter.

"What's that?" one of them asked.

"What?"

"That . . . thing." Their unsteady footsteps came nearer to us. "It's hay!" Sergei exclaimed. "What's it . . . look, there's more."

"Where are we?" Viktor asked. "It looks like . . . a circus! We've stumbled into a circus!"

Boris yelled to them, "You've got an hour. You can either stay at your circus or come over here, but please shut up, whatever you do."

"Yes, comrade, straight away," Sergei said, giggling.

"If you fall off that hay and break something, you can stay here and rot."

"You can stay here and rot," Viktor repeated, mimicking him. I held tight to Zasha, frightened they would continue their exploration.

Suddenly, in full voice, Sergei began to sing. "*Oh, Mother Russia, the land of my birth. . .*" Before I could get a word out of my mouth, a moan came out of Zasha's.

"What was that?" Viktor asked, slurring his words.

"That was me, singing like a bird."

"No, it. . ."

Again, Sergei sang: "*To walk in your forests, in your fields so full of grain. . .*"

"Zasha, no," I whispered frantically. But her snout was up and she was singing along.

"I heard it! What is it?" Sergei cried.

"A wolf!" Viktor said in a stage whisper. "Maybe this is a wolf's den."

"I hope it is," Boris snapped. "Wake me when they've eaten you both."

"Didn't you hear it?" Sergei asked, with a tinge of fear in his voice.

I clamped my hands over Zasha's furry snout. "No, girl. They'll find us. They'll kill you." She moved her head back and forth, not liking what I was doing to her.

I heard what sounded like Sergei jumping off of his hay bale. "Maybe Boris is right," he said in his drunken way. "Just an hour and we'll be on our way."

"Wait for me," Viktor responded. "It's dark."

As Sergei and Viktor made their way back to Boris, Sergei sang softly, as though to himself, "*Hold me to your heart, Mother Russia*."

This time Zasha howled loud and long as she broke free of my awkward grasp. There was a commotion among the men; they talked over one another in their fear and confusion. The one sentence I heard clearly was "Where's my gun?"

There was only one way out of the little box canyon besides the entrance through which they'd come, and that was along the rocky streambed.

I peeked around the wall of the cave. It was too dark

to see them, which meant they couldn't see me, either. "Zasha, come." I bent over and ran; Zasha was close behind. The men were still yelling and telling one another what to do as we came within a few metres of the creek, ready to run to the left and follow it to safety.

"Give me the torch!" Boris demanded. I saw its yellow light hit the base of the hill on the other side of the water, zigzagging wildly in its effort to locate the source of the sound.

Just as we were about to sneak around the craggy edge of the outcropping where the stream cut through, I felt the light upon us. It took all my willpower not to stop and turn towards it.

"Oh my God!" I heard Sergei cry. "It's a wolf – and a wolf boy!"

"It's not a wolf, it's a dog, you idiot, and a boy," Boris said.

"A dog!" Viktor exclaimed. "Let's get him! I claim that dog as a present for my Anya."

"You'll have to catch it first," Sergei yelled, "or it's mine!"

"*Whooooo!*" It was a war cry from Viktor. I could hear the stamping of their racing feet as they began their hunt for us.

"Come back, you two! If you get lost, you're on your own." There might only have been Sergei and Viktor after us, but as my father warned me many times, "Steer clear of the drunken man; you never know what he might do."

I ran as fast as I was able, but was slowed again and again by muddy piles of branches and rocks left on the ground when the water overflowed its banks after heavy rains. Zasha shadowed my every move.

It was a kilometre to our farmhouse as the crow flies, through open land still cluttered with plant debris from the last harvest. There was nothing to hide us, not even a tree. But I couldn't lead them to our home, where my family might be put in danger.

"Owww!" I heard one of the men scream.

"Get up, Sergei! I almost tripped over you."

"I'm trying. Give me the torch, I'm in the lead."

"Here."

I turned around, staring into blackness pinpointed by a shaky golden light. Where to go? Where?

The creek ran north, but in another hundred metres curved to the right and on to the property of our neighbour, Mr Golovin. He had three strong sons, all named Alex, after him. They were wild boys who loved to fight over the slightest thing. If I guided the men to their house, the Golovin boys would surely take care of them.

No. Someone had said, "Where's my gun?" I had to assume at least one of the men chasing me had a gun. It would be deadly to lead two drunken, armed men to the Golovin farm.

"Here, doggy! Here, doggy, doggy!" Viktor called.

"Hey, kid." It was Sergei. "We don't want to hurt you. We just want to talk to you."

I kept running, deciding on a risky manoeuvre, but it was the best plan I could come up with. When the stream began to bear right, I'd make a sharp left, run to the far western barrier of our property, and then turn south to hide in the workers' shelter.

As drunken and clumsy as Sergei and Viktor seemed, they were still grown men and trained soldiers. They were gaining on us; I could tell by the nearness of their voices.

"Are you sure we saw what we saw?" Sergei asked.

"Of course. And I want that dog."

"It's mine."

"Not if I find it first." They laughed, and I knew then they wouldn't give up till they found us.

The bend in the channel was within sight. "Come on, Zasha," I whispered, and ran to the left across the field. Here and there, broken stalks still stood, eerie in the dark, moonless night. Then I remembered. There was a small marshy area on the farm, about two hundred metres away. My father had filled it again and again with dirt, but still the water returned. It was surrounded by a mud so thick my father called it quicksand, even though it wasn't exactly that. But if you waded into it, very soon you'd decide to turn back as you felt it grab at your every step.

The trick would be for me and Zasha to get to the other side of the marsh, let them know we were there, and then hope they ran straight for us and into the paralysing mud. Oh, yes, and hope they didn't shoot us in the process.

How would I get them to follow me where I wanted? The simplest answer was usually the best – I coughed.

"Oh! There he is!" Viktor yelled, even though I knew they couldn't see me, and the torch was pointed in another direction. I coughed again.

"That way! Over there!" Now they were on our trail. This was how Petr died, I remembered as I ran, protecting Zasha from thieves. I was determined I would not meet the same fate.

We dashed through the ragged field, across two of the roads that cut through the farm and into the area near the marsh. Zasha and I were both panting by now. I looked straight in the darkness for the landmark that would help me locate it: an old bath that the cows used to drink from. We hadn't had cows for years, but we gathered the rainwater that collected there.

"Where is it?" I muttered. It was easier to see out here

in the open than it had been in the hilly area near the water, but it was still inky black.

"Give up, kid. You can't beat us." I think it was Viktor. He sounded like the adventure was starting to make him mad.

On my left, finally, I saw the outline of the old bath. It marked the near end of the small marsh. Now I just had to lure them to this area and get to the other side. Taking Nikolai's piece of fire-making steel out of my pocket, I ran to the bath and pounded on its metal side four times, and then raced to position myself on the opposite side of the marsh from them. Zasha kept up with every step.

"Did you hear that?"

"There, over there."

I glanced over my shoulder long enough to see that the torch was coming in exactly the right direction.

"Anya, my darling," Viktor yelled, "the doggy is almost yours!"

"Not quite," I muttered, using all my strength for the final sprint. Once there I could see the outline of the bath because the torch was aimed directly at it. They approached the edge of the marsh, which in the dark looked the same as the surrounding land. I stood still and, waving my hands in the air, said, "Over here!" I waited for the torch to find me. It hurt my eyes, but I looked straight into its glare. "Come and get me!" I yelled, then turned and bolted for the workers' shelter that was at least another two hundred metres away.

"You crazy kid!" one of them cried.

"Get back here. I order you. The army orders you!"

"Then let the army come and get me!"

I knew they would head straight for us. All sorts of cursing and swearing followed my answer to them. Not ten seconds later, I heard one of them say, "You'd better say your prayers, because when we catch you we're—" and then it stopped.

I knew they'd be ten or twenty metres into the marsh and mud would be pulling at them, surprising them with its strength, with its suction. The tone and volume of their voices changed, and without hearing the words as the distance between us grew, I was sure that they were asking each other what on earth they had walked into, and all attention would be turned to extricating themselves from the slimy, wet quagmire.

Zasha and I had escaped. Just for luck, we didn't stop until we reached the western edge of our land, then turned north for home.

CHAPTER ELEVEN

We entered through the back door and ran as quietly as we could up the stairs to the second floor. The light in my mother's room was still on. The door was open ten centimetres or so, just enough so that I could see her standing by her dresser, reading what looked like a letter and crying.

"Mama!" I said, pushing the door open. "Is everything all right?"

"Oh!" she said, pressing her left hand against her chest. "You scared me. Nikolai said you would be late; I thought I should wait up. Where were you?"

I respectfully ignored her question. "What's wrong?"

She folded the paper quickly, slipped it in her pocket and brushed her tears away. My mother rarely cried, and the sight of it distressed me.

"Is it Papa? Did something happen to Papa?"

She shook her head, picked up a wooden hairbrush

from her dresser and began running it through her hair. "No, Mikhail, everything's fine."

"It's not fine," I challenged her, emboldened perhaps by my success in evading the army men. "Please show me the letter." I stood tall, certain that the letter would confirm my worst fears – that my dear papa was dead. Better to face it than to live in the fear and dread that had pursued me since he left to fight.

"It's not a letter. Now go to sleep. Everything's fine."

"Mother, I'm his son. I deserve to see that letter."

She stopped brushing her hair and sighed. "It's not a letter—"

"I saw it with my own eyes, please, Mama, don't—"

"—it's a poem."

"What? A poem?"

"Yes. Your father sent it to me two years ago, along with a letter." My mother looked so young for a moment, with her hair down and her face lit by the faraway memory.

I walked closer to her. "May I see it?" She nodded with a quick smile and pulled the much-worn paper from her pocket.

"Did he write it?" I asked, unfolding it.

"No, another soldier wrote it. But many soldiers and

many soldiers' wives have copies of it." I began to read the poem out loud. It was called "Don't Look Away".

Remember the summer we fell in love?
The kiss as we floated on the lake,
When you declared my eyes bluer than a June sky?

Think of my eyes now.
Don't look away;
Not for anything.

Pay no attention to the bombs that fall around me;
Ignore the bullets;
Believe they have another destination.
Hold me in your unflinching gaze
So that I, too, am blind to the devastation.

If I notice the guns,
They will notice me.
If I look at the dead at my feet,
I will join their ghostly ranks.
Let me feel your strength, your soul
Shining there for me in your eyes,
Or I will perish.

With each line it was more and more difficult to speak because my throat was tight with emotion and my eyes blurry with tears. My mother joined me from memory as I choked out the last few lines.

Don't look away;
Not for anything.
And I will come home
To row with you again on that tranquil lake
And declare my love a thousand times,
With eyes the colour of a June sky.

I threw myself into her arms. "Oh, Mama! You don't believe he's dead, either."

She stroked my hair as we cried. "No, my son. I don't. I can't."

I pulled away from her to look into her face. "I know he'll come back to us. He has to."

Zasha nuzzled close to us, putting her paw on my mother's leg. We laughed and wiped our faces. "Oh, Zasha," she said, petting her. "What a good, good dog you are." She sat down on a chair next to the bed. Zasha whimpered loudly and pawed at my mother's leg so hard that she said gently, "Zasha, you're hurting me."

"Down, Zasha," I commanded her, secretly happy to have

an excuse to show my mother how well trained she was.

Zasha not only lay down, she rolled on her back. I laughed and rubbed her belly. "Good girl. She likes it when I do this." I looked up at my mother, who had a strange expression on her face. "Mama – what is it?"

"Move your hand, Mikhail." I was confused but did as she asked me. She bent down and ran her hand gently across Zasha's stomach area several times.

"What's wrong? What is it?"

She didn't answer immediately but finally said, "Nothing's wrong. Zasha is going to have puppies."

"Oh!" I gasped. "How do you know?"

"I can feel them."

"Show me." She took my hand and guided it so that I could distinguish small mounds from the general softness of Zasha's belly. "When will they come?"

"It's been so long since I've seen . . . soon?"

I sat back on my heels. "What are we going to do?"

"I don't know, son."

"How will we. . ."

"I don't know."

"What if someone finds out that. . ."

"This is a problem we aren't going to solve tonight," she said, getting up from her chair. "It's very late. We'll talk to Nikolai and Rina in the morning."

I felt so frightened that I turned around one last time as I was leaving her room. "You won't make us give her away, will you, Mama?"

"Go to bed. And feed her a little extra in the morning."

CHAPTER TWELVE

Zasha lay quietly on the floor, next to my bed, warm and secure in a nest of old blankets – like the one in the kitchen that Rina had made. I couldn't sleep after my conversation with my mother. To know that she, too, was waiting for my father made me unbearably sad. It made us both seem like foolish dreamers, people who couldn't face reality. It almost undermined my belief that he would come home one day.

I turned on to my side, staring out of the open window. Stars filled the sky. So Zasha was going to have puppies. This, too, should have made me happy. Instead, it doubled my fears for Zasha's safety.

How many puppies would she have? I wondered. Three, four, six, seven? How long until they were so big they needed their own homes? Would they bark? Of course they would, I thought, and then everyone would know about Zasha and her babies. If some crazed citizen didn't kill them out of patriotic duty, the men in the yellow van would descend upon us like an avalanche that destroys everything in its path. I tossed the blankets off me and sat up, breathing hard.

"Mikhail, what is it?" I heard rustling from Nikolai's bed but couldn't see him in the dark.

"I'm sorry. I didn't mean to wake you."

"What's wrong?" I heard a scratch and then saw the flare of a match. He lit the squat candle we kept on the nightstand for the times when the electricity went out, which happened often in the winter.

Zasha leaped on to my narrow bed and settled next to me. "Zasha's going to have puppies."

"That's wonderful news! How do you know?"

"Mother told me."

Nikolai swung his feet on to the floor, leaning across the space that separated our beds, and patted Zasha.

"Good girl. Let's keep them all. It will be fantastic."

"You must be talking in your sleep, because this puts the puppies and Zasha in danger."

"Why does it have to be like this? The war is over!"

An idea began to form as we sat there in the candlelight. "Can you see the clock? What time is it?"

Nikolai stretched around to see the little clock on the other side of the room. "I think it's almost four. It will be light soon."

"Good," I said. "Blow out the candle and turn on the light."

"No, that hurts my eyes."

"Close them, then. And get dressed. We're going on a visit."

"What are you talking about?" he asked as he blew out the candle. When he turned on the small lamp that sat on the nightstand between us, we both groaned and closed our eyes.

"Do you remember what Katia said? There is a man not far from here who is going to start a kennel."

"Yes. So?"

"We need to go there and have a look."

"Why?"

"He may be able to help us."

"Don't be silly. We need to stay away from him."

"No. We need to find out what he's planning to do. Katia said he had only a few dogs. Now that we know Zasha is going to have puppies . . . we have something he may want. Don't you see? It could keep Zasha safe."

"What are we going to do when we get there? Knock on his front door and announce that we have a dog we're trying to hide? He might steal her from us."

"We're not taking her with us, if that's what you're worried about."

"I certainly hope not. But what exactly are we going to do?" Nikolai pulled on his boots as I fumbled in a drawer for a warm shirt.

"We'll look around, see what he's built, what he's got planned."

"Will we introduce ourselves?" Nikolai asked, this time sincerely.

"Not yet. Let's just see what we can find before he gets up. Maybe we should go to the village afterwards, hear what people are saying about him."

As I finished lacing up my shoes, I glanced one last time at Zasha, who sat watching us curiously from my bed, looking almost concerned. "Don't worry, girl," I said, patting her head. "We'll be back in time for breakfast." I closed the window and the bedroom door to make sure she wouldn't follow us.

Nikolai guided Paku quietly out of the barn. We rode together, he in the front and I behind. At fifteen and thirteen, our combined weights equalled one grown man; Paku didn't complain. When we reached the paved road that ran in front of our house, Nikolai said, "Katia said he's at the old Orlov place, right?"

"Yes. Let's cut through the back pastures instead of going all the way around on the main road." I knew Paku was happier walking on soft ground, and it would be at least a fifteen-kilometre round-trip – more, if we went into the village afterwards.

Our little corner of Russia, being so far north, had missed most of the terrible events that destroyed so many farms, and families, in the 1920s and '30s. In the richest and most fertile lands in the south, the government had taken farms away from their owners and put them under the control of the state. It had resulted in a terrible famine when Nikolai was a toddler.

As the years passed, practicalities began to replace theories, and farmers in our part of the world carried on as they had for centuries. True, the state sometimes told us what to plant and hired workers for us, but our farm had never been taken over. The Orlov place had been occupied by the government for seven dreadful years. The once-productive dairy farm had been poorly run and badly treated by those who had no personal interest in its success. Eventually, it was abandoned: the Orlov family never returned. This was the first time in my memory that someone was living there.

After almost an hour of riding, Nikolai and I jumped off of Paku to give him a rest. He grazed for a few minutes and let us walk him – with a stop for a bite here and there in the last kilometre.

Fence posts still stood along the southernmost property

line of the Orlov farm, but many of the cross boards were gone or fallen at one end. "This is it," I said, stopping in the hazy dawn light. "What should we do now?"

Nikolai looked around thoughtfully. "I think we should tie Paku's reins to a tree and explore that building." He pointed to the right, to a long building with a high roof, the type where cows are usually milked. It wasn't a barn exactly, but that's how I thought of it.

I nodded my agreement. "That looks like the house up there." I pointed to a dilapidated two-storey structure to the left, far in the distance.

"He won't be able to hear us," I said, "but let's try not to be seen." Nikolai nodded his agreement.

We tied Paku to an oak not far from the barn. Climbing through a large gap in the fence, we moved quickly towards it. The grass was long and thick; a twisted runner caught on my shoe and I stumbled. The door hung loose on its hinges; Nikolai went in first. The floor was cement and the first sound we heard was the crunch of glass under our shoes from one of the many windowpanes I could now see were missing.

We walked slowly. On the right were stalls where the individual cows used to be kept and milked; on the left, an open area with scraps of hay still scattered over the floor.

"I can see why he chose this building to turn into a

kennel. These old stalls are perfect. You could probably divide them in two and still have plenty of room in each one for a dog."

Nikolai nodded. "But it's in terrible shape. How is he going to pay for all the repairs that need to be done?"

"And where will he get the dogs? And what kinds, I wonder?"

"Hey, look at this!" Nikolai bent down and picked up something shiny off the floor.

"What is it?"

He blew off a little dust and rubbed it with his thumb. I stood nearby and watched over his shoulder as he cleaned it up. "I think it's a piece of a—"

"Don't move!" a deep and loud voice behind us yelled. "Put your hands on your heads and turn around." My heart beat so hard, I could practically hear it. We turned around slowly, as asked, hands on our heads.

About twenty metres from us stood a man with only his trousers and boots on, his curly dark hair a tangled mess. He was well muscled and aiming a military rifle at us.

"Who are you?" he barked. "Why are you here?"

Nikolai and I exchanged frightened glances.

"I am Mikhail Tarkov," I said in a higher than normal voice, "and this is my brother, Nikolai."

"And?" he demanded.

"And we're here because . . . because we heard you were going to open a kennel."

"And we like dogs," Nikolai added eagerly. The rifle stayed aimed at us.

"Is anyone with you?"

"No," we answered in unison. "Just our horse," I added.

"How old are you?"

"I'm thirteen and my brother is fifteen." My arms were aching. I think they might have been shaking, too.

"We're sorry, sir, for having invaded your property like this," Nikolai said in his most proper voice.

"Yes, we're very sorry. May we go now, please?" I thought I saw a flicker of a smile pass over his face, but I couldn't be sure because the gun and the scope covered so much of it. He slowly lowered the gun to reveal a weathered face with a scar on the side of his cheek near his left ear.

"Don't ever come snooping on the land of a soldier. You could get yourselves killed." He stared at us, seeming to take in every detail. "You say you like dogs?"

"Yes, sir," we answered. I was sure now my poor arms were turning to stone.

"Have you had breakfast?"

"No, sir," we said.

"Come on, then." He waved us towards him with his rifle. "I was just about to have some tea." Long ago my father taught us never to argue with a man if he had a gun in his hand. I wasn't about to start now.

We followed him out of the barn to his run-down farmhouse. I don't think you could say we really had a choice.

CHAPTER THIRTEEN

"Careful of the step," he said, which was good because the entire right half of it was missing. "And you – go and catch some mice," he told a skinny tabby cat who was reluctant to leave her spot by the back door. The screen door, which was full of holes, creaked when it opened and banged when it closed.

We passed through a small pantry and into the kitchen. It was immediately clear that no woman lived in the house with him. The windows were covered with years' worth of dust and water stains. I guessed that every dish he owned was either on the counter or in the sink, all of them dirty. The floor looked like it hadn't been swept since the Orlovs left years before. He leaned his rifle against an old icebox.

"Sit down," he said as he pulled a cigarette out of an almost empty pack and lit it. "Oh – did you want one?" He held the pack out towards us.

I shook my head; Nikolai said, "No thanks."

He shrugged. "A little young, perhaps. But I saw German boys your age in Berlin, all soldiers. Tea?"

"Please," I said, remembering my mother's teaching that you always say yes to someone's hospitality, no matter how humble. The man opened cupboards, looking for extra cups, I assumed. They were mostly empty, although I thought I caught a fleeting glimpse of a mouse.

I watched him as he moved. He didn't seem embarrassed that he didn't have a shirt on. His muscles looked so hard and tight, they almost scared me. Or maybe it was the scars that marked him. I stole a glance at Nikolai, who was examining him as intently as I was.

The cigarette dangled from his lips as he said, "Aha!" and turned towards us holding up two cups he'd dug out from the pile in the sink. He ran the water and rinsed them well, but there was no soap. He didn't dry them before pouring tea into them from a pan on the stove. "It should still be hot. There's no sugar."

We murmured our thanks as he set the cups in front of us. He grabbed his chair at the top, turned it around, straddled it and folded his arms across the top. He flicked the ashes from his cigarette on to the floor.

"Tell me what you've heard."

Nikolai was taking his first sip of tea, so I answered. "About what, sir?"

"Dimitri. My name's Dimitri."

He pointed at me. I said, "Mikhail." Nikolai gave his name quickly. The gun was nearby, and we were eager to please.

"Tell me what you've heard about a kennel." He inhaled his cigarette deeply, held it for a second, and exhaled it in a long stream.

"Not much," I said, shrugging and showing my open hands. "Just what our friend Katia told us."

"Is she the one from the newspaper?"

"Yes."

"I thought her name was Irina."

"Oh, she's the real reporter," Nikolai said. "Katia's the editor's daughter who trails along behind her."

"Ah, yes. The little girl who asked too many questions."

I tried not to smile. The truth is, I liked Dimitri, even if I did meet him at the wrong end of a gun. It made me bolder than I should have been. "What kinds of dogs are you going to raise?"

He looked at me closely, examining my face, not answering my question. Finally, he said, "Tell me what it is you like about dogs."

I glanced at Nikolai, who still seemed nervous. Taking a deep breath, I said, "Everything. I like the way they feel, I like the way they look. I like their smell. No one is more loving or loyal. They're strong and smart. Some of them are even funny." I stopped for a moment, gazing out of the dirty window. "They make a family complete. That's what I like about them."

"And you?" He nodded towards Nikolai.

"I agree with what Mikhail said, but for me, one of the best things about them is that they want to work." He laughed self-consciously, as if we might consider that answer stupid. "I mean, if you've ever had a sheepdog, you know that the dog lives to herd those sheep. He wants so much to please his master, and to do a good job. He's very depressed if he can't work!"

Dimitri listened closely. "Under what circumstances is it acceptable to hit a dog?"

Nikolai said, "Never. Our father taught us that animals can think and feel. He forbade us ever to be cruel to one."

"So you are vegetarians, then!" he said in a mocking tone.

"Our father called it one of the great contradictions of life that you treat animals respectfully, but also survive by eating them."

"A wise man, your father." Dimitri leaned back and put his cigarette out by throwing it in the sink. "Where is your father now?"

"We don't know," I said, trying to drain my voice of emotion. "We haven't heard from him in two years."

"A soldier?" We nodded. He raised his eyebrows and made a clicking sound out of the side of his mouth. "Men are still coming home. He could be anywhere. A relocation camp, a hospital. . ."

"But wouldn't he have written to us?" Nikolai asked, his concern obvious.

"Do you have a family?"

"A mother and a sister."

"Be thankful for what you've got. That's my motto." He got up abruptly and said, "Come with me. I want to show you something." By this time I was no longer afraid of him, and Nikolai didn't seem to be, either. He walked through a dusty parlour with little furniture, out of the front door, down the steps and towards a small building that I guessed was once a laundry house.

"Hello!" he called out when we were about ten metres from the entrance. In response, I heard the whimpering of dogs, and finally a welcoming bark or two as he opened the door.

Inside, uncaged, were six dogs – the mangiest, most ragtag bunch of dogs I'd ever seen. They greeted him like the Messiah, standing on their back legs, wagging their tails, running in tight circles, jumping in the air.

"OK, down, my boys and girls," he said, touching each one, petting them, patting them. "That," he said, pointing to a Doberman pinscher with part of its right front leg missing, "I got off a dead German soldier. This little dachshund showed up at my barracks one night half frozen; he's cross-eyed and a little slow. Those two I call the Old Folks," he said with a nod towards two small black-and-white dogs. "They stay together always and communicate in a language all their own, like an old married couple. They're mutts."

"What about this one?" Nikolai asked, pointing to a fierce-looking grey dog.

"That's Schatzi; he's a schnauzer. I traded two bottles of vodka for him. The black one next to him was given to me by a Gypsy. He's some kind of terrier."

"Given? By a Gypsy?" I was incredulous because Gypsies were well known to drive a hard bargain.

"And beautiful she was. Call it a goodbye present." He laughed to himself.

"What are you going to do with them?" I asked.

"Breed a superdog! That's what they expect."

"Who are 'they'?"

"The army, of course. Those idiots killed half the dogs in Russia, and now they realize their mistake. There are no dogs left in Russia! Or not many, anyway. How am I going to. . ." He stopped talking as if frustrated, or maybe a little embarrassed at revealing his emotions.

"What do you mean when you say they killed half the dogs?" I asked, wanting to know the truth.

He knelt down to get closer to the dogs without answering. Nikolai and I did the same and were rewarded with licks and dogs trying to jump in our laps and running under our legs. Nikolai laughed when the Doberman knocked him off balance. With every minute he spent with the dogs, Dimitri seemed calmer, as if this might be the only place he was truly comfortable.

"Was there fighting in your village?" he asked us finally.

"No," I said, "but it got close. We could hear it sometimes."

"Then I'll just say this: the dogs – used by all the armies, not just ours – were as brave as any soldier. They took messages across battlefields, they sniffed out the location of men we thought we'd lost. They died in huge numbers. And then some genius decided we should kill all the dogs bred in Germany." He shook his head, as if he could barely tolerate the memory, and stood up quickly.

"As you can see, three of these dogs are German dogs – the Doberman, the schnauzer and the dachshund. Suddenly, the army doesn't care. Let me tell you, Rommel had a perfect dachshund, Hitler had a beautiful German shepherd. I'd give my left arm to have dogs like that, no matter how much I hate those miserable—" He broke off and cleared his throat. "But they don't exist. I haven't seen a dog in Russia except my own for months.

"So," he said, stretching out his arms towards his dogs, "I will have to make my superdog with the help of this brood."

"How many females?" Nikolai asked.

"Precisely one." He pointed to one of the Old Folks. I looked down so he couldn't read my face as I thought of Zasha and the puppies she was expecting. He walked to the door and held it open for us. "Now I have to compete with dog thieves and Gypsies. They're combing the countryside for dogs and selling them for huge profits."

"Dog thieves?" I repeated, thinking of the men in the yellow van who had cornered us in the barn.

"Any dog at all is worth its weight in gold. Do you know anyone with dogs?" he asked us as an afterthought.

"No," I lied. He led us back towards the house.

"If you hear of any, tell me. The army will pay a good price, and we treat them well."

"Of course," said Nikolai, looking as anxious as I was to get away from there before Dimitri somehow figured out our secret.

He turned towards us when we reached the stairs to the house. "You should go. Your mother will be looking for you."

"Thank you for the tea," I said as we turned to go left, around the side of the house.

"Oh, one more thing," he said. We stopped and looked back at him. "Soldiers are observant. We have to be; our lives depend on it." Neither of us spoke, not sure what he was trying to say.

"Both of you have dog hair all over your clothes."

I felt a fearful rush of adrenaline up my neck. "It must be from your dogs."

"Yes, all six of them," Nikolai said with a forced cheerfulness.

"I noticed it in the kitchen, before we went out back." Of course, I thought, feeling panicky; Katia brought the hairs she found on Petr's coat to Dimitri. He's the one who thought they might have been from a German shepherd. Why had we ever come here?

"You are mistaken," I said as I began to walk away. "We have no dog."

As soon as we were out of Dimitri's sight, we ran as fast as we could back to Paku and rode to the safety of our farm.

CHAPTER FOURTEEN

"Where were you?" my mother said, standing up from the long pine table in the middle of the kitchen and coming towards us. "We were worried!" Rina nodded in agreement, her mouth full of brown bread. Zasha sat at Rina's side, under the table, waiting for bites of anything my sister wanted to share with her. She ran to us, and as we patted her she smelled with interest the scent of the dogs we'd just been with.

"We're sorry, Mother," I said. "We left early to do some exploring."

My mother looked at us incredulously. "You don't expect me to accept that as an answer! Out late last night, then you disappear again at dawn? Sit down. I'll make you breakfast while you tell me exactly what the two of you were doing."

"We're not hiding anything from you," Nikolai said, pulling out a chair. "It was early; we didn't want to wake you."

"There is such a thing as a note. Now tell me where the two of you have been."

Nikolai and I exchanged a glance. As my mother heated up the pan for our eggs, I said, "Katia Klukova came to see us again. That's why I was so late last night. She almost caught us with Zasha, out by where we built the hiding place for her."

"You're becoming quite expert at avoiding my questions."

"No, Mama, it's about what Katia told us. She said there was a man living at the old Orlov place. . ."

"The Orlov place? No one's lived there for years."

"We went there this morning to see if what she said was true, and it is! It's dilapidated and dirty, although he doesn't seem to mind." Being a woman who prized cleanliness and order, she scowled in a disapproving way. "Anyway, he's going to start a kennel—"

"To breed a superdog!" Nikolai interrupted. "And he's got six dogs already, all shapes and sizes."

"A superdog?" Rina said. "What does that mean?"

"It means we've been idiots, using our dogs to fight our wars and to kill others." I said it with such vehemence that all of my family members turned to look at me in surprise. Zasha gazed up at my face, her head tilted to the side, as if questioning me.

"What it means," Nikolai replied quietly, "is that our poor country needs guard dogs, and working dogs and . . . and every kind of dog, and he's going to help breed that new dog. A new Russian dog."

"Are you going to tell him about Zasha?" Rina asked solemnly.

"No. At least not for a while. Did you tell her, Mother?"

"Tell me what?" Rina demanded. "What happened?"

"Nothing bad," my mother said, setting plates of eggs and bread in front of Nikolai and me. "Zasha is going to have puppies."

"Oh, hooray!" Rina cried, clapping her hands together like the child she was. "Can we keep one, Mama? Oh, please. Just one. It will be so cute. Maybe we should keep two so they won't be lonely. Yes, just two, Mama, just two."

My mother sat down, her elbows on the table, holding her head between her hands, palms pressed against her forehead, ignoring her daughter's question. She had been strong when my father was called to war, and was still hopeful after two years of silence. She had managed to grow enough food and trade for what we didn't have to keep us alive. She'd thought of all sorts of ways to scrape together more money, like renting Paku out to neighbouring farmers and making hats that kept ears from freezing until there was no more yarn or fabric to be had.

Now, on this beautiful summer morning, it seemed that one more problem might make her crumble.

All of us stopped eating, eyed one another nervously, and stared at my mother. "What is it?" Nikolai asked gently. I thought of my mother as she was the night before – poem in her hand, waiting, hoping, the force that kept our family together.

She shook her head and sat up straight, taking a deep breath. "What are we going to do with puppies? This is not a game, children. Zasha . . . Zasha's not even ours. We should have told the police about her."

"No, Mama, you know what could have. . ." I said.

"We don't know anything."

"I do. I know what I saw in Leningrad," Nikolai said solemnly. "Two beautiful German shepherds shot dead in the street."

My mother sighed, as if she didn't have an answer for him, but continued. "Once the puppies are a few weeks old, we'll have to find homes for them. Then everyone will know about Zasha and what we have done."

"The problem is not yet a problem," Nikolai said, quoting what my mother often said to us. A smile flickered across her face. He stood up and walked over to put a hand on her shoulder.

"We look at where we are, what we know, and

we make our plans from there," I chimed in, again paraphrasing her advice. "You said we have a few weeks before we have to worry about what to do with them?" She nodded. "So what problem do we have today?"

"Katia," Rina said with a mouthful of bread before anyone else could answer.

"Oh. Yes." That stopped me, because Katia was persistent. The thought of how she almost caught us with Zasha sent a chill through me.

Nikolai chewed on the corner of his lip as he stared into the distance. "We need to annoy Katia," he said. "Make her want to leave us alone."

"How?" I asked, listlessly pushing eggs around on my plate.

"Rina and I will pay her a visit." There was a gleam in my mother's eye as she said it.

"Really?" That got my attention. "And do what?"

"She's been here twice in the last week or so. We'll have to help her understand that each of her visits will result in a long and uninteresting return visit from Rina and me."

Rina looked at her doubtfully. "Uninteresting?" she repeated.

"I'm afraid so. We'll stay well past the time that good manners say we should leave. In fact, for every one visit she makes, we will pay her two."

"I thought you didn't like Mrs Klukova," Nikolai said, slipping into the chair next to her.

"Of course I do. Although getting a word into her conversation is sometimes challenging," she added with a laugh.

"Mrs Golovin said Mrs Klukova clucks so much, you'd expect her to lay eggs."

"Rina!" my mother exclaimed, unable to hide the laugh in her voice. "Don't speak that way of your elders."

My sister shrugged. "I'm sorry, Mama. I was just saying what Mrs Golovin said."

"That's what we'll do," my mother said, slapping the table for emphasis and looking like herself again. "Rina, go and get the ribbons Katia brought you. I'll plait your hair and tie the ends with them. Nikolai, go to the chicken coop and see if we have a few eggs to spare for Mrs Klukova." She started to get up from the table.

"Mama," I said, "that's good, I'm glad you're going, but there's something that can't wait."

"What?" She sat back down tentatively.

"We have to decide – now – where Zasha will give birth. You said yourself the puppies could come soon." I broke off a piece of bread and fed it to Zasha under the table. "I think there's no question Zasha has to give birth here in the house or in the barn, but there are no hiding places in the barn. We've looked." My mother laced her hands around her teacup and waited for me to continue. "She has to have somewhere she feels safe, where there's enough air and light, where she can come and go, and where it's warm." I sighed deeply, wondering how we were ever going to find such a perfect place.

"Is there somewhere under the house?" Nikolai asked doubtfully.

"Too risky. She might come out any time a visitor came, to protect her pups," my mother answered.

"The cave is too exposed, and too far away," I said, thinking out loud and remembering the drunken soldiers. "There could be predators that would eat the pups."

"Don't talk like that!" Rina exclaimed.

Nikolai stood up. "It's perfectly clear. It has to be somewhere in the house." He walked quickly out through the hall and into the living room. The three of us followed, much more interested in solving the problem than in finishing our breakfasts.

CHAPTER FIFTEEN

We stood in the oblong living room with its many windows. If you were a boy, you could have hidden under the sofa cushions if you were still enough, or behind a china cabinet if you were slim. But there was no hope here for a dog and her puppies. The same was true with a small parlour on the other side of the front door; no cupboard, nothing but exposed, empty space.

Gathering in the roomy entry hall with its high ceiling, we looked around us. If you faced the stairs that led to the second floor, the door to the kitchen was on your right, the living room, front door, and small parlour behind you. Next to the stairs, on the left was a large cupboard, and to the left of that a hall that led to the back bedroom where Petr died. Next to the bedroom was a back door and another door that took you to the far end of the kitchen. You could make a complete circle by walking down the hall, past the bedroom, going into the kitchen, out the other end of it, and into the entrance area where we stood. We did just that, with Zasha at our heels, twice, ending up in front of the closet with no answer.

Rina said, "We're doing it all wrong." She got down on her hands and knees. "Now I'm Zasha's size. I'm going to look at the world like she does." She moved on all fours to the cupboard, opened the door and crawled in. We'd already looked in the cupboard, of course. As overstuffed as it was with winter coats and boots, there was no hiding place. Rina came out, now sniffing like a dog. Zasha nudged her playfully with her nose and pawed at her side. She headed for the stairs to the second floor.

"Rina, get up," my mother told her. "You'll tear your dress."

"I say let her stay like that," I said, running past her up the steps.

"Here, Rina, here. Good dog," Nikolai said, pretending to hold up a treat in front of her. "Sit, girl!" Rina was unperturbed and continued her climb.

"Leave her alone and concentrate," my mother said, as she, too, passed Rina.

When you reached the top of the stairs, there was a linen cupboard to your immediate left. It was on top of, and the same size as, the one in the hall below. I peered in; it was filled with extra blankets, quilts, towels and sheets. If you went a little further, you entered our one and only bathroom. It was larger than most in old farmhouses like ours. The floor was covered with tiny white tiles that made it look clean and inviting.

Now, if you turned around and went back the way you came, you'd see the door to my parents' bedroom. Turning right, going down the hall, and then right again: on your left, Rina's room; straight ahead was the bedroom I shared with Nikolai.

My mother, Nikolai and I went in and out of the bedrooms a few times, as if we would discover something we'd missed if we only looked harder. Zasha stuck close to me. Rina continued crawling and sniffing her way through the rooms, which was seeming a lot less amusing and a lot more annoying, until I heard her call, "I found it!" The three of us came running to find Rina on her feet and holding open the door to the linen cupboard. My shoulders slumped.

"Rina, we've all looked there. It won't do; they'll be able to see her." Nikolai started to walk away. Even my mother looked disappointed.

"You haven't heard my idea yet," Rina said confidently.

I was tempted to follow Nikolai, but my mother said, "Tell us, then."

"It's simple. The cupboard downstairs is very tall. How high is the ceiling, Mama?"

My mother thought for a second. "Three metres, I think."

"And it's right below this cupboard. All we have to do is make a new ceiling in the cupboard downstairs, maybe a metre lower than the real one—"

"Oh," I gasped, knowing just what she was thinking.

"This is my idea, Mikhail. Let me finish. Then, we build a trapdoor from this floor," she said, pointing to the floor of the linen cupboard. "Then Zasha will have a space a metre high, and – what do you think, Mama? – about a metre by two metres?"

Nikolai was on his knees examining the floor. "Brilliant. We'll put the hinges on the inside of the door so they won't show."

"We can keep it open when there's no one around so Zasha won't be all closed in," I said.

"I'll drill airholes in the floor. Mother can hang things from the ceiling of the closet downstairs to distract attention from its height."

"And the holes," I added.

My mother nodded. "I will stuff it with hats and scarves, anything awkward or bulky so it will naturally feel crowded without seeming suspicious."

"Rina!" I said. "I could almost kiss you."

"Well, don't," she replied, but her smile betrayed her pride in figuring out our problem.

I knelt down next to Nikolai and examined the floor. "It's oak," I said. "It will be very hard to cut."

"Maybe for you," he teased. "Leave it to me; it's a man's job." I pushed him playfully; he laughed and pushed me back.

"All right, you two. We may as well get started now. This could take longer than we think; there may be problems. . ."

"It's perfect, Mama. There won't be problems," Rina assured her.

My mother, who'd seen many a problem in her life, put her arm around her daughter's shoulder. "Let's go and see if one of the Golovin boys is going into town this morning. They can take us to Katia's." Everyone knew any one of the three wild sons would welcome an excuse to go into town and get out of his farmwork.

"Good idea," Nikolai said seriously, without looking at them, already focused on the work to be done in the house. "Let's clear out this cupboard, Mikhail, and decide how to begin." I was grabbing a pile of blankets almost before he finished his sentence, anxious to create a place where Zasha could nestle in peace and bring her pups safely into the world.

CHAPTER SIXTEEN

It wasn't nearly as simple as it seemed. A floor between a first and a second storey is not just a thick board. It is a structure made of beams, with a space of fifteen centimetres or more in between the ceiling on the first floor and the floorboard of the second floor.

Nikolai and I were inexperienced carpenters, much more comfortable in a field or a classroom than with tools in hand. We began our work in the cupboard on the second floor after clearing it out and removing the shelves so we had room to stand and work.

Our first job was to take out the floorboards. Whoever built the farmhouse had done an exceptionally good job. The boards seemed hard as stone, and so tightly laid together that it took us what felt like hours before we were able to remove our first one. Even then we struggled not to crack them near where they were nailed down.

Nikolai and I sat in the dimly lit closet catching our breath. "Zasha could have her puppies before we get this done," my brother said, looking down at the small area missing its covering of oak.

"There's no other answer. We have to do this." After a moment I added, "I'll bet if Papa were here, he could figure this out for us."

"If Papa were here," Nikolai said with a sigh, "he'd be brave enough to defy the whole world. He'd take Zasha walking out in the open and dare any man to challenge him." He picked up a crowbar to prise out another narrow strip of wood.

"Why aren't we doing that?"

"I don't know. Because we're not men yet. Because we have Mother and Rina to think about. Because we don't know enough about the world to be certain we could keep Zasha, or that no harm would come to her."

"You're practically a man," I offered. "I'm just thirteen."

Nikolai laughed. "At last you admit I am a man and you are a puny child."

"Hey," I said, pushing him playfully, "that's not what I meant."

"Prove it, then. Remove all the floorboards yourself."

"Give me the other crowbar and we'll see who the man is."

It was just three hours later that the metre by two-metre cupboard was stripped bare of all traces of an oak floor.

“Now comes the hard part,” Nikolai said, looking over the thick crossbeams that formed the support between the ceiling below and the floor we’d removed. I was tired and the muscles in my arms hurt, but I didn’t want to admit that to Nikolai.

“What do we do next?”

“We have to cut around the edge of this cupboard, through the beams, and through the ceiling of the cupboard below.”

“But you have to kneel on it to cut it. Won’t it collapse and drop you down to the floor below?”

“I was hoping to avoid that,” he joked.

“Maybe I should get on a ladder downstairs and start sawing, too.”

“Why don’t you go to the barn and see if the saw blades are rusted. Look for some long nails, heavy ones, and some hinges.” I was relieved to be out of the closed space, and ran to the barn.

All of our tools, implements, and odds and ends were stored on shelves in the far corner of the barn. I sorted through several glass jars filled with screws, nails, washers and other miscellaneous bits of materials. The supplies were skimpy and uneven; nothing had been replenished since the war broke out, when almost anything made of metal disappeared from the shelves. The nails I found were small, rusted, and slightly bent – nothing that would support our design for a hiding place for Zasha.

The saws needed scrubbing with a wire brush, and a thin coat of oil; it took about fifteen minutes to finish. When I was finished, I found Nikolai at the kitchen table having cheese and bread. I helped myself to some and told him between bites, "We don't have any nails or hinges."

"Can you go into town and buy some?"

I nodded. "Anything else I should look for?"

"Not yet," Nikolai answered. "It's better if we go there in several small trips . . . not arouse any suspicions."

I took a container marked *Flour* out of a cabinet near the sink and put it on the kitchen table. It was where my mother kept a small amount of money for household purchases. I hoped what I took would be enough for what we needed. Zasha walked me to the front door, acting very much like she wanted to go. "No, girl," I said, kneeling down and scratching behind her ears. "You may not be going out again for some time. Would you call her, Nikolai?" I asked. "I don't want anyone to see her when I open the door."

"Zasha, kitchen!" he cried, and she obeyed, trotting off to join him. Being careful was a habit that was already paying off, I learned, as I opened the front door and saw my mother, Rina, and Alex Golovin pulling up in front of the house in the ancient van Mr Golovin held together with baling wire, ingenuity and a dose of magic.

Rina jumped down from the back and bounded up the stairs two at a time. "You're not going to believe what I saw!" she said breathlessly, and ran past me into the house. I followed her like a dog after its master.

CHAPTER SEVENTEEN

Rina held the kettle under the tap and carried it with both hands to the stove once it was full. "Tell us!" I insisted, having waited patiently while she washed her hands and helped my mother set out cups for all of us to have tea. Rina looked proud, as though she were glorying in the last moments of holding her special information.

"Katia has a secret," she said teasingly, and waited for us to ask her for more.

"What is it?" Nikolai demanded. Rina glanced at my mother and they shared a quick smile.

"Well, we went for our visit, and when we got there Mrs Klukova was home, but Katia wasn't."

"Where was she?" I asked nervously, picturing her roaming our farm for clues that would lead her to Zasha.

She shrugged. "I don't know, but Mama and me decided in advance what we would do if she was gone."

"And that was. . ." I wanted to turn her upside down and shake her to make her words come out more quickly.

"I said to her mother, 'Mrs Klukova, I have something for Katia. May I run up and put it in her room?'"

My mother joined in, unable to hide her smile as she said, "Mrs Klukova nodded her head yes so there would be no interruption in her conversation, and she never stopped for a breath until Rina had come back down and we were almost ready to leave."

Nikolai looked like he was losing his patience until Rina said, "Her room is like a . . . what is the word you said, Mama?"

"Shrine."

"A shrine to dogs."

I was dumbfounded. "What do you mean?" Nikolai and I leaned closer to her, as if we hadn't heard her correctly.

"She can draw really well, and there were pictures of dogs everywhere. Mostly in pencil, but some in ink, and even some in paint, but you could tell she'd drawn them all herself." Rina sat back, looking satisfied to have been such a capable spy.

"What else?" I asked, trying to make sense of it.

"They had names. She put a name under each dog. The one she drew the most was a little black dog, Mr Buttons."

"Mr Buttons!" Nikolai laughed. "Who would give a dog such a name? Zasha – now *that's* a good name for a dog." Zasha turned towards him at the sound of her name. The water boiled in the kettle and my mother poured it over the same tea leaves we'd used at breakfast, a trick we'd learned when tea became scarce.

"This makes no sense," I said, staring at Rina. "She was so . . . angry when she told us of her suspicions that Petr had a dog with him."

Rina shrugged again. "All I know is that there were three little stuffed dogs on her bed by her pillow. It looked like she made them, or maybe her mama did." Nikolai and I gaped at each other in amazement.

"I think it's perfectly clear," my mother said calmly. "She hoped Petr had a dog because she wanted that dog for herself."

"Well, she's not getting Zasha," I said darkly, folding my arms in front of my chest.

"Maybe we could give her one of the puppies," Rina said. Nikolai turned to her immediately, like she'd suggested we give her one of our own arms.

"She said our whole family would be *traitors* if we had a German dog!" he fumed.

"And that it would be destroyed. Should be destroyed!" I added, standing up. "This makes Katia even more dangerous. She's not investigating Petr's death as a good citizen. She's doing it for her own selfish reason: she's desperate to have a dog."

"That's rather sad, don't you think?" Rina asked.

"No!"

"But look how happy Zasha has made us."

"You don't understand," I snapped. "You didn't see her out there sniffing around for Zasha like a bloodhound. Nikolai, I'm going to town now to get the things we talked about. If Katia comes anywhere near our house. . ." I was breathing heavily at the very thought.

"Mikhail," my mother said in a voice of warning. "Do not speak rashly of what you might do."

It was all I could do to answer, "Yes, Mama," before I ran to the barn to harness Paku for our trip into town.

CHAPTER EIGHTEEN

The wind in my face and the slow, steady rhythm of riding Paku was the perfect antidote to the fear and anger I felt after hearing Rina's story. I tried my hardest to feel compassion for Katia, thinking of her making drawing after drawing of Mr Buttons, a dog she clearly loved and missed. But mostly I felt like I wanted Katia to move far away, to Moscow maybe, or Siberia would be even better, where she would never again think about, talk about, or be anywhere near Zasha.

It wasn't easy shaking Katia out of my thoughts and refocusing on what I needed to do in town. Poor Paku had to work a little harder than usual, because I made him trot part of the time. The thirty-kilometre round-trip would take too much time if we walked the entire way, and I was eager to get back home to help Nikolai with Zasha's hiding place.

In our village there were still hitching posts along the sides of the streets. I tied Paku to one of them and went into the hardware store, where everything from knives to coffee pots was sold. I filled a scoop with nails; Nikolai had said to get half a kilo. There were only two types of hinges. I chose the one that could be hidden on the inside of the trapdoor.

As I left the store, I felt drawn towards the newspaper office of the *Vasily Reporter* just two doors down. Something told me this might be my only chance to talk to Irina alone and find out what she knew. If Katia was with her, well, I wasn't sure what I would do.

The noise hit me like a wave as soon as I walked in. People talking, arguing, shouting into telephones, competing with the rumble that came from somewhere in the back where the paper was actually printed.

No one seemed to be in charge; everyone was busy at their desks as if in their own worlds. It took me a minute to locate Irina because her back was to me. When she turned around, I walked over to her quickly.

"Miss Irina, I'm Mikhail—"

"Of course!" she said, interrupting me. "I've been thinking about you, in fact. I need to talk to you."

"You do?" I said nervously. "Why?"

"Come outside," she said, steering me towards the front door. "Oh, the noise!" She shook her head as she closed the front door behind us, then breathed deeply.

"Everyone's in an uproar about the German soldier who was found in Tikhvin."

"A soldier? This far north?"

"Hiding in a barn, half starved. He was happy to see the police after the beating the villagers gave him!" She laughed.

I don't think she would have laughed if she could have seen inside my heart and understood how frightened this news made me for Zasha's sake. Did wars ever truly end? I wondered.

"What did you come to see me about?" she asked.

After hearing about the soldier, I didn't want to talk to her about Petr. Thinking fast, I said, "Dimitri Moravsky told me you paid him a visit."

She seemed startled, and I thought I caught the flash of a blush in her cheeks. "Really? What else did he say?"

"Not much. He talked about his plans. . ."

"For the superdog?" She laughed again.

"You don't think it's possible?"

"Possible, yes, but not with that bunch of strays and rejects he's got." Her words seemed harsh, but she said them almost tenderly, as if she was deeply touched by his plans.

"I think he can. He'll just have to be patient, and have some luck."

"Luck?" She looked at me sceptically.

"Luck that other dogs will come his way."

"Hmmm, I suppose so."

"What do you know about him?"

It seemed for a moment that she was deciding whether to answer me or not. "He's what we might call complicated."

"What does that mean?"

She looked ahead, out past the town as she spoke. "He spent part of the war in jail."

"Why?" I couldn't imagine him as a criminal.

"He attacked an officer who was whipping a horse. It took three men to pull him away, is what I was told." She glanced at me, and we shared a look that showed our unspoken respect for his action.

"What else?"

"An orphan since he was fifteen. Lied about his age to join the army. He was a sharpshooter. They sent him into the most dangerous places, alone, with only a rifle."

I pictured everything she told me clearly, as if I were seeing it at the cinema. "Amazing. Did they still let him be a sharpshooter after he attacked the officer?"

"No. That's why he's here with his crazy collection of dogs. That's his new assignment – far away from the officers! But the man who told me all this, who used to be in his unit, says Dimitri likes animals better than people anyway."

"Who can blame him?" I said with a laugh, thinking of Zasha. "Animals are not our equals; they're our superiors!"

"Maybe." She smiled a faraway smile. "An intriguing man."

"Is he . . . all right?"

"What do you mean?"

"He seems a little nervous, and I saw lots of scars on his body."

"How did you see his scars?"

"He had his shirt off."

"He did?" I had the feeling she wished she would have been there with us. "I've just met him once. He seemed like he had his wits about him. But maybe nervous, as you say. The war did terrible things to people. A lot of the men who've returned aren't the same as they were when they left." We walked quietly for a few moments. "Did you lose anyone in the war?"

"Four of the fathers of my friends at school died. Many more, if you count uncles and brothers."

"But no one in your family?"

"My father has not yet returned."

She stole a look at me. "Communications are very bad all over the country." I nodded, hoping she'd drop the subject. She must have read it in my face, because she said, "I have some news!"

"What's that?" Almost anything seemed preferable to talking about my father.

"I found Petr's wife!" My heart felt like it stopped.

"How?"

"He'd sewn his personal information into the hem of his coat."

"Did the police find it?"

"No," she said proudly. "I found it. They checked his pockets and shoes, but I know that people sew money and valuables into their clothes. I felt around his garments until I heard the crinkle of paper, and there it was: Petr Gribovich. He lived sixty kilometres away; I wrote to his family. His wife is coming here tomorrow to collect his remains." *Oh*, *Zasha*, I thought, trying not to let myself feel what it would be like to say goodbye to her.

I nodded and stared at the ground as we walked. "That's why you wanted to talk to me? To tell me his wife had been found?"

"Yes, but I wanted to talk to you alone, to see if there were any more details you could remember." She stopped walking as we came to the end of the paved sidewalk, where it turned back into a well-worn path of hard-packed dirt.

I gazed up at her and, with all the innocence I could muster, said, "No. It was very simple, and very quick. I don't think he spoke at all. He was really ill. My mother wrote it all down for the police."

She watched me as I spoke, pushing her hands deep into the pockets of her sweater. "It's just . . . something is not right. I have a feeling about it that I can't define."

"I don't know what you mean."

"It's what makes us reporters," she said with a little shrug. "We follow our noses rather than our heads sometimes."

"Are you thinking he may have been murdered?" I asked, thinking maybe I was the one who was missing something.

"I don't know. His wound was not a murder wound, and yet he died from it. I think he was probably the victim of an attempted robbery."

"Or maybe a successful one."

"Yes! Very possibly. I want the whole story. I'm hoping to get more pieces of the puzzle from Mrs Gribovich."

We turned around and walked back towards the newspaper office.

"Does Katia know about this?"

She gave a sigh of frustration before she caught herself. "I'm sorry; I know she's your friend."

"I know her, but I wouldn't say we're friends."

She seemed relieved. "I don't know how her father gets away with giving her details about our stories and forcing us to take her with us."

"Can't you say no?"

"Not if I want to keep my job."

"Does she know that you found Petr's wife?"

"No," she said with a look of glee, "and you mustn't tell her. Unless she's going through my personal files, she won't know until after the meeting is over. Are you sure there's nothing else?" she asked again.

"We've told you everything."

"Oh, I almost forgot. She wants to meet you."

"Mrs Gribovich? Why?" I said, fear seeping into my bones.

"Because you're the one who found him and last saw him alive." Surely she would ask about Zasha. My heart felt heavier than the bag of nails I carried.

"What time?"

"At noon at the police station. You can bring your mother if you like."

I nodded and forced myself to smile. "Certainly. I would be happy to be there." I don't think there was a sadder boy in all of Russia at that moment.

*

"What's wrong?" Nikolai asked as soon as he saw me when I finally returned home.

"Petr's wife is coming to the police station tomorrow at noon. She wants to talk to me."

Nikolai closed his eyes and sat down wearily next to the pile of flooring we'd spent hours tearing up. "What are we going to do?"

"We're going to lie."

CHAPTER NINETEEN

Nikolai and I lay in our beds that night, neither of us able to sleep. Finally, I lit the candle on the low table between our beds. Even Zasha seemed restless, getting up every few minutes to paw at the blankets on which she lay.

"I think she's trying to make a bed for her puppies," Nikolai said, reaching down to caress her. She glanced up at him, made a moaning sound, and tried again to find a comfortable spot.

"You think Mother's wrong about the timing?"

"She could be. Who knows? I think we should be ready from today onwards for her to have her puppies." He sighed and sat up. "There is so much more work to do on her hiding place."

I couldn't think of that – what was the point? This might be the last night she slept under our roof.

"Oh, Nikolai. What are we going to do tomorrow? I don't care what I said before: I can't lie to Petr's wife. What will I say when she asks about Zasha?"

He was silent for a moment. "There is only one question we have to ask ourselves."

"And that is?"

"What would Papa want us to do?"

"Yes. What would Papa want us to do? That's perfect. . . But, what *would* he want us to do?"

"He taught us never to lie, so you must tell the truth."

"I can't believe you would say that! We lied to the men in the yellow van, didn't we?"

"Yes."

"And we lied to Dimitri."

"That's true."

"And to Katia."

"She doesn't count. Does she?"

"I think Papa also tried to teach us not to be foolish and let people take advantage of us."

"Then it's simple. We don't offer information. If she asks us something, we answer truthfully."

"Isn't that a way of being dishonest?"

"I'm not sure. I think we should watch and listen carefully before we go blurting out everything we know."

"It all feels so wrong. I know I can't look her in the eyes and lie. She lost her husband. Maybe his dog would be a great comfort to her. Maybe she loved Zasha, too." A lump appeared from nowhere in my throat.

Nikolai sounded as sad as I felt when he said, "Even if we have to give Zasha back, maybe we could give her back after she has her puppies."

"And not tell Petr's wife about them?"

"Yes. Maybe."

"I suppose, but isn't that stealing? If Zasha is her dog, then the puppies belong to her, too."

Nikolai blew out the candle with a deep, harsh breath, not bothering to ask me if I was ready to try to sleep again. I heard him punching his pillows and rearranging himself on his bed. "I wish you'd never found her," he muttered.

"What?"

He repeated it loudly, and I heard his tears. "I wish you'd never found her!"

CHAPTER TWENTY

When my mother heard about Petr's wife, she insisted the entire family be present at the meeting. There was one point on which we strongly disagreed.

"We have to bring Zasha with us," she said. I felt frantic at the thought.

"No. I'm not going to expose Zasha to all those people in her condition."

"We can't keep Petr's dog now that his family has been located."

"If you make me do that, I will run away from home and never come back!" I had never spoken to my mother so disrespectfully before. It shocked us both, and we stood for a moment, speechless, looking at each other.

In my fear and frustration I barely noticed Nikolai, who'd run into the kitchen, until I heard him say, "Someone's coming!"

"What?"

"Someone's coming – I heard them. Where's Zasha?"

My mother answered. "She's upstairs with Rina." Turning to me, our anger forgotten, she said, "What are we going to do?"

The front door, which we'd forgotten to lock, flew open and in rushed Dimitri Moravsky. He couldn't get the words out of his mouth fast enough.

"Where's the dog?"

We stood frozen, silent.

"Where's the dog?" he repeated loudly, almost desperately.

"What do you mean?" I asked.

"This is no time for games. They came to my house. They tried to steal my dogs."

"Who? Why?" I asked, still in shock from his arrival and his demand.

"Thieves. Dog stealers. Because they can sell them for a fortune on the black market."

"Did they get them?" Nikolai asked, looking tense and fearful.

"What did you do?" I asked, speaking at the same time as Nikolai.

"I shot at them," he said, in a deadly calm voice. "You don't come to the house of an army man and expect to take his property."

My mother gasped. "Were they hit?"

"I didn't aim to kill, or they would be dead now. They left in a hurry, and without my dogs."

She put her hand over her heart and closed her eyes. "Did they fire back?"

"Yes."

"They were in a yellow van, weren't they?" I said.

"Yes!"

"They've been here before. They're coming back." I could barely breathe.

"Whether you admit it or not, there's a dog here. If I know it, and even that little girl suspects it, then others do, too."

"You mean Katia?"

"I don't know her name," he said impatiently. "The one from the newspaper. She's been talking to everyone, pretending to investigate."

"But—"

"We're wasting precious time. Give me the dog. I'll keep it at my kennel. They won't come back a second time." All of us stood silently and then looked at one another uncertainly.

I heard Rina come down the stairs saying, "Mama, what's going on?" I prayed she'd left Zasha upstairs. As she came into view, I saw she was alone.

"It's your decision, Mikhail," I heard my mother say, as

if through a fog. I thought of Zasha, of how I loved her, of how much a part of our family she was already. And I remembered the men in the yellow van, and the one with a pole and a leather collar on the end of it for catching dogs.

"Come with me," I said, turning and running up the stairs two at a time. Dimitri and Nikolai followed. We moved quickly down the hall. I took a deep breath and, hoping I was making the right decision, I opened the door to our bedroom.

There sat Zasha, two or so metres from the door, her ears up, her body tense and ready for action. I heard Dimitri gasp. The three of us entered the room.

"This is Zasha," I said proudly, full of love, full of fear.

"Zasha," he repeated. "You are the most beautiful German shepherd I have ever seen." He stood as if transfixed. "You may be the most beautiful dog I've ever seen."

"And she's clever," Nikolai added. "We've trained her to do all sorts of things." Dimitri nodded, still gazing in amazement at Zasha.

"And she's going to have puppies," I said. "Soon." Dimitri looked at me and blinked, as if he hadn't heard me right.

"We have to get her out of here. Now." We hurried down the stairs, Zasha at our heels. My mother and Rina followed us out to the front of our house, where Dimitri was parked. He opened the side door to his old, rusted jeep. I knelt down next to Zasha.

"You have to go with Dimitri, Zasha. Be good. And we'll be back to get you very soon." Tears filled my eyes. "Now go!" I motioned towards the vehicle; Zasha didn't move. "Zasha!" I cried. "Go!"

"She needs help," Dimitri said softly. "The puppies in her belly are too big. The jump is too high."

I rubbed my nose on my sleeve. "Will you help me?"

The two of us struggled to lift Zasha into the jeep. She was unsettled by it, reaching out repeatedly to steady herself, making the job even harder. *Why are you placing me on a narrow, battered seat a metre off the ground?* she seemed to be asking.

"There," Dimitri said, shutting the door and running around to the driver's side. Zasha and I exchanged one long, last look.

"When do we get her back?" I asked, not caring who saw my tears now.

"I don't know. As soon as it's safe." He was starting the reluctant engine and roaring away before I could say, "Goodbye, my Zasha. Goodbye."

CHAPTER TWENTY ONE

Nikolai and Rina weren't at all certain I'd made the right choice. "How do you know you can trust him?" Nikolai demanded.

"And what if we never see Zasha again?" Rina asked accusingly.

"Tell me again what you know of this man," my mother said, sitting at the kitchen table. Zasha's sudden departure had upset her, too.

But Dimitri was right. We hadn't been back in the house more than five minutes when I heard the deep rumble of a truck approaching. "Wait here!" I cried. "Nikolai, make sure the door is locked." I ran to the window in the living room and recognized the yellow van immediately. The driver was the same brute I remembered, with his pale-eyed sidekick in tow, but there was also a third man. They were out of the van almost before it stopped and walking quickly towards the front door. "It's them!" I shouted and dashed into the hallway where my mother, Nikolai and Rina huddled close together, looking scared and unsure of what to do next.

"Open up!" someone shouted as he pounded. "Open up! This is official government business." The front door shivered with each blow from his fist.

"Who are they, Mikhail?" my mother asked, fear in her eyes.

"Thieves."

"They say it is official business."

"They're liars," Nikolai said angrily. "They've been here before."

"What? Why didn't you—"

"Mother!" I said loudly, trying to calm her down and get her to focus on the danger on the other side of the door. "Dimitri said the men have guns. What should we do?"

I saw the strength and determination return to her eyes. "Get three hunting rifles out of the cupboard. Quickly." Nikolai and I had them out in seconds, along with a box of shells.

"Rina, as soon as the guns are loaded, I want you to unlock the door and then run and get behind the three of us."

"Open up or we'll break it down!" I heard one of the men yell as I finished loading one rifle and handed it to my mother.

"Just a minute!" my mother called back. "I'm coming." The pounding ceased. Nikolai and my mother stood ready, guns aimed at the door. I put in my last shell, snapped my rifle shut and joined them. Rina tiptoed to the door; her left hand was on the lock, her body already turned away for escape, her eyes on my mother.

Rifles raised, our eyes pressed against the scopes, my mother said, "Unlock it, Rina." I heard the click of the latch; Rina moved so fast to get behind us, she was a blur. The unsuspecting men came rushing through the open door only to screech to a halt in front of the three guns aimed at them.

"Down!" my mother shouted. "Down on the floor! Hands on your heads!" They hesitated as if they couldn't comprehend what they were seeing.

"You've got two seconds to get down or we shoot," Nikolai said. Two of them dropped immediately to the ground. The big man was still assessing the situation, not quite so ready to give up. "If you're not down on the floor in one second, you die." I guess the man decided not to test him, because he complied with a curse and a groan. It was a wise choice. Our father had made sure we were expert marksmen, training us from the time we were five or six years old. My mother, who trained with the women's home militia, wasn't as good as we were, but she was still a solid shot.

"Rina, go to the barn. Bring me the rope hanging on the wall near the goose pen. Hurry!" Rina spun around and ran through the kitchen and out the back door.

"Silence!" my mother thundered when two of the men began to speak quietly to each other. Two minutes went by without a sound. My whole body ached, my shoulders and arms felt like they were full of a thousand tiny needles. Where was Rina? All she had to do was grab the rope and run back. The men were getting restless; I could feel it. I was afraid that in a few more minutes they would decide to take their chances with a woman and two boys. For all they knew, our rifles were empty. The truth is, we hadn't fired those rifles for a long time, maybe even a year. They could easily have failed us if we were forced to fire.

"Two of you were here before," Nikolai said. I think he was having similar fears and stalling for time. None of them answered. "We know who you are. You're dog thieves."

"No, no, no," the big man said, trying to sound sincere. "We're from the army. We pay for dogs. We have plenty of money. How much do you want?"

Without moving the rifle away from the firing position, I responded. "First, we don't have a dog. Secondly, you're not with the army; you're common criminals. Thirdly, we know you've already tried to steal the dogs at the kennel." Just as I finished speaking I heard the back door slam, and Rina came in as quickly as she could, carrying a heavy circle of rope.

"I'm sorry, Mama, I—"

"Not now," my mother said sternly. "Nikolai, I want you to take the rope and tie up the one on the left. Hands behind him, wrap it around the waist, and then tie his feet together. Leave enough slack so he can walk."

I didn't like my mother's idea. Nikolai was the tallest and strongest, but it put us in a vulnerable position. If the man decided to fight, the other men would surely attack the three of us. It was also clear that we couldn't stand there indefinitely with our guns raised, no plan and no rescue party on the way. But I had to trust her and not let the men know there was any dissension among us.

"Rina, take Nikolai's gun," she continued. "And you – scum lying on the floor – listen well. My daughter will put a bullet through your hearts as fast as my sons. If any of you makes even one sign of resistance, we all shoot. Understand?"

There was some mumbling from the men. "I can't hear you!" she shouted.

"Yes," they all said loudly.

Before Rina could pass the rope to Nikolai, the big man began talking. "Madam, this is all a misunderstanding. If you'll just give me a chance to—"

"Stop talking!" she yelled.

"—explain why we came here today." He'd taken his hands off his head and was beginning to push himself into a sitting position.

"Get down! Get down now!" He continued to move slowly while talking in a low, conciliatory tone. I knew that in another moment he would try to grab one of our rifles: there would be bloodshed.

My father's voice pounded in my head: "Mikhail, never use violence if it can be avoided. But if your family is threatened, defend them with your very life." I knew what I had to do. Flipping my rifle around, I struck the man hard on the side of his head with the wooden butt of the gun.

He moaned and grabbed his head and, with an angry glance at the four of us, he lay back on the floor and put his hands behind his now-bleeding head. Within a second of hitting him, my rifle was back in place, ready to fire if he moved again.

Then I heard something that almost made me lose my focus and put down my rifle – Dimitri's jeep. Seconds later, the sound of footsteps on the stairway was greeted by curses and sounds of frustration from the men on the floor. Dimitri ran through the open door so fast, he almost tripped on one of the men's feet.

"Don't shoot!" he said to us with a smile, a gun in his right hand. "It's me!"

"Dimitri!" Nikolai cried with relief.

"And who are these fine gentlemen?" he asked as he bent over to feel their pockets and take the weapons hidden in their jackets.

"You!" he barked at one of them, letting him know who he meant by giving a not so soft tap against the man's backside with his foot. "Get up. Keep your hands on your head. Turn around." The man did as he was told. "Mrs Tarkov," he added politely, "would you be so kind as to ask your daughter to hand me that rope?" Dimitri took the rope from Rina, put his gun in his waistband, and pulled a sizable knife from a sheath on his belt to cut the rope.

"Children," he said derisively to the man as he tied his hands behind his back. "You let *children* take you prisoner. Now you!" he commanded one of the other men with another swift kick. Dimitri repeated the procedure, but also tied the two men together with about half a metre of slack rope between them. He finished tying up the third man in the same way, all three of them now linked by rope and unable to escape or fight.

Dimitri stopped to light a cigarette and then talked while holding it in place with his teeth. "Now," he said, holding up the keys he'd taken from one of them. "We're going to see what you've got in the back of that van. You three go first. I'm right behind you and will shoot you if you try to run." The men looked scared, as if they knew he meant every word.

"Mrs Tarkov, boys, follow me. You, too, Rina," he added as she peeked around from behind my mother. "Keep your guns ready. Stay alert."

"Go!" he shouted at the three men. They shuffled awkwardly down the stairs, cursing and complaining as they repeatedly bumped into one another. Nikolai, my mother and I followed, our guns still raised.

Dimitri unlocked the back doors of the yellow van and opened first the right side, then the left. I couldn't believe what I saw.

Half of the van was full, stacked floor to ceiling with cages. Each cage contained one dog: thin dogs, fat dogs, small dogs, dogs too big for their cages who could hardly move. They looked so frightened that not one of them made a sound, but simply stared back at us. Finally, a little brown dog in the front whimpered and walked in a little circle in his cage. All of us stood motionless, in awe of the unbelievable sight.

"I ought to shoot you all now and save the government the cost," Dimitri said, throwing his cigarette to the ground. "Where did you get these dogs?" He said it softly, as if making a concerted effort to keep hold of his temper. When no one answered, he yelled it. "WHERE DID YOU GET THESE DOGS?"

"We bought them from their owners," one of the men said unconvincingly.

"Good. Then you'll have receipts and names and addresses, and they can all be accounted for."

"Well, we—"

"No!" Dimitri said, holding up his hand as if to stop the man's words. "Don't tell me. Tell the police."

"We haven't done anything wrong!" one of the men offered. "No need to involve the police. We can work this out between us. How much do you—"

"Shut up and get in," Dimitri snapped, waving his rifle towards the open door. The three of them looked almost comical as they struggled to climb up into the back of the truck while tied together. They finally stood next to the edge of the van and slid in on their stomachs, mumbling and arguing with one another.

Before he shut and locked the door, Dimitri told them, "If even one dog is hurt, killed or suffers in any way during our drive, I will do to you exactly as you have done to them." Then he locked them in tight.

"Nikolai, can you drive?"

"Yes, sir."

"Take your mother and your sister with you. Follow us to the police station." He threw the keys to Nikolai, who almost dropped his gun trying to catch them, but looked delighted.

"Mikhail, you'll ride with me in the jeep." Within sixty seconds we were on the road, headed to the police station. The only way I could have been any happier was if Zasha were at my side.

CHAPTER TWENTY TWO

We caused quite a stir on the streets of Vasily that day. The yellow van and jeep drew attention on their own, because so little petrol was available that most villagers had gone back to using horses and carts.

But when three men tied together half stumbled, half fell out of the back of the van, with four guns aimed at them, people seemed to appear from nowhere to stare in wonder.

Three policemen rushed out of the front door of the station to greet and assist us. "What happened?" asked the grey-haired police captain I remembered from our last visit.

Dimitri smiled proudly. "This good mother and her fine sons captured these dog thieves through their quick wits and bravery."

"And me, too!" cried Rina.

"Forgive me, princess. How could I have forgotten you?"

"Dog thieves," the captain said with some scepticism. "I didn't know there were any dogs left to steal."

"Have a look for yourself," Dimitri answered, opening

the back of the van. The policemen looked shocked as they gaped at the dozen or more cages and their cargo of scared, silent dogs.

"My goodness," the captain whispered, taking off his hat and scratching his head. "Who do they all belong to? Where could they have got them from?"

"That's for you to work out, my friend," Dimitri said, slapping him on the back good-naturedly. "Now where do you want these three?"

The captain refocused on us, which was a relief because my arms had held up a gun for just about as long as they were able.

"Oh, oh," he said, slightly flustered, "bring them this way. Ivan, you and I will go first. Lev, you follow behind. Make sure no one gets away." I almost laughed, wondering how far he thought they'd get tied together like three monkeys.

Once we were inside, the policemen briefly questioned each man, then took them to one of the two cells in the back, out of sight. Dimitri wrote a statement of events for the police captain.

I noticed the captain reading, frowning, looking up at me, and then continuing with his reading. The time for telling the whole truth was upon me. If the captain didn't know the whole story, I was sure much of what he read in Dimitri's statement wouldn't make sense. I had turned to look for Nikolai when I saw Irina coming through the door with a woman I didn't recognize. She was an older countrywoman with a worn face and a scarf covering her head. Even though it was July, she wore a warm coat that fell past her knees.

"Oh, no," I said aloud, and looked at the clock high on the wall in the back of the room. It was noon. I'd completely forgotten that I was to meet with Irina and Petr's wife.

"Mikhail, hello!" Irina greeted me. "I see you brought your whole family. How nice."

"Well, I, you see. . ."

"This is Mrs Gribovich, Petr's wife."

"I am very pleased to meet you," I said, slightly bowing my head. She didn't answer, but smiled just enough that I could see she was missing some of her teeth. My heart was so heavy, I walked like the dead when I followed Irina and Petr's wife over to a table.

"I'll be with you in a minute," I heard the captain tell Irina, "just as soon as I've finished here." Irina, Petr's wife, and I sat down to wait.

"This is the young man who found your husband," Irina said kindly, touching the woman's arm. Mrs Gribovich reached in her pocket, pulled out a rumpled handkerchief and pressed it firmly against her right eye and then her left.

"Thank you," she said so softly I almost couldn't hear her.

This was the moment when I had to tell her about Zasha, too. It was now the time to let go of a creature I had come to love as I loved my family; the bond was undeniable, unbreakable. I opened my mouth to speak, but Irina beat me to it.

"I don't know if you want to look at this now," she said, pulling something from a large satchel. "But the police let me take a picture of Petr. We didn't know who he was then, and we were going to make handbills with his picture on them to see if anyone could identify him."

Mrs Gribovich nodded and pressed again at the tears in her eyes. Very gently, slowly, Irina pulled a black-and-white picture of Petr from a large envelope. She handed it to Mrs Gribovich. "This is for you to keep."

Petr's wife stared at it for a long time. "Who is this?"

"What?" Irina asked.

"Who is this man?"

"That's Petr. Your husband," Irina answered, sounding confused.

Petr's wife held the photo in her left hand and slapped it with her right. "This is not Petr. You said you found my Petr."

"But the name Petr Gribovich was sewn in his coat with your address. That's how I found you."

"This is not my husband!" she said loudly. "Don't you think I'd recognize him? Someone must have stolen his coat. Or maybe he sold it."

"Sold it?" I said.

Mrs Gribovich looked up at me, and then at Irina. "Petr liked his vodka. He was always selling our things to get some."

Irina looked dumbfounded. "I am so sorry. I should never have jumped to the conclusion that just because the name was in his coat he was—"

"But he told us his name was Petr," I said, feeling bad for her. Irina shook her head and closed her eyes. "That could have been his name, too, or – maybe he bought the coat, as Mrs Gribovich said, and pretended to be its owner for reasons we'll never know."

Irina smiled at me appreciatively. "Thank you, Mikhail." She sighed. "I should have been more careful; I got carried away by my own cleverness. I apologize again, Mrs Gribovich. I am so very sorry."

"When did you last see your husband?" I asked her.

"About three and a half years ago."

"Why did he leave?"

"He was going to try to cross the ice road to Leningrad. His sister was there. He wanted to get her out."

Even I knew what this meant. She would probably

never see her husband again. The Germans had surrounded Leningrad for two and a half years. Although some supplies and people did make it in and out on the frozen waters of Lake Ladoga, many more had been starved or killed.

"Have you reported him missing?" Irina asked.

"No. Everyone in our village knows he's gone."

"Let's give that information to our police captain, just in case."

"I'll get him," I said, and walked quickly over to his desk. But I had something very different in mind.

CHAPTER TWENTY THREE

"Sir, may I speak with you?"

"Certainly, young man."

"Privately." He came out from behind his desk and walked with me to the back of the room, where no one could hear us.

I stared at the floor for what seemed like a long time, thinking of my father and how he would want me to act. With an image of him in my mind, I lifted my head and looked the captain directly in the eye. "I have been honest with you, sir, in what I've said to you." I paused. "Except for one thing."

He nodded slowly, giving me his full attention. "Go on."

"Petr had a dog with him when I met him. He called her Zasha. We took care of her like we took care of Petr."

I waited for a response, but when none came, I continued. "This dog is the most beautiful dog in the world, but she is a German shepherd." I could feel my emotions rising in me like a tide. "I know what people have been doing to German shepherds. It's so wrong. She's innocent. All dogs are innocent." I had to stop for a moment so I wouldn't cry. It helped that I remembered something the captain didn't know.

"Miss Irina showed the picture of Petr to Mrs Gribovich, and she said it was not her husband."

He looked surprised. "Oh, I see," he said, as though he was putting all the pieces of the situation together.

"My family and I kept Zasha because we didn't want to see her hurt or killed. I apologize for not telling you earlier."

"Where is this dog now?"

"At Dimitri's house. Those men came to steal Zasha," I said, motioning generally towards the cells.

"How did they know you had a dog?"

"I don't know," I said, uncertain of the answer. "They came twice. I think they knew because Katia Klukova suspected Petr had a dog."

"The editor's daughter?" A look of surprise passed over his face.

"Yes, sir."

"Why did she have this suspicion?"

"She saw hairs on his coat when we brought him in here after he died. She said you told her she could take some and try to find out what they were."

He looked embarrassed. "I was just indulging – that is, I never dreamed. . ."

"Dimitri said she went around the village asking everyone about a dog and whether they'd seen us with one. So much so that those men arrived at our door. At least, I think that's how it happened."

"So, you withheld evidence."

"Yes, sir."

"And you didn't tell us all the details of your experience."

"No, sir."

"Your mother knew and approved of your actions?"

"Please don't blame my mother. It was me. I loved Zasha. I couldn't let her go; neither could my brother or sister. And my mother is so kindhearted, and so sick of war, and we haven't heard from my father in two years. . ."

"All right, all right," he said, touching my shoulder as I grew more upset. "You obviously know Dimitri Moravsky."

I nodded, breathing deeply, trying to regain control of myself.

"The army has given him the great responsibility of developing a new dog. A Russian dog, a dog who can guard, and fight, and work, and herd – all the things dogs do."

"It's very exciting." I smiled for the first time in what seemed like hours. "The men came to steal his dogs, too, before they came to our house."

"So I've heard."

"He's the reason Zasha is safe. And alive. Oh . . . there's one more thing."

"There's more?"

"Zasha is going to have puppies very soon." Then the police captain did something that completely shocked me: he hugged me and laughed.

"This is great news! Oh, how I've missed all the dogs. Do you know we used to get angry here when we saw them roaming the streets? Now I'd give anything to see them again."

"Did you ever have a dog, sir?"

"Yes, many. But our last dog died just about the time the war started. Since then, they've all but disappeared. Dimitri!" he cried suddenly, raising his right hand to get his attention. Dimitri was talking to Irina and Petr's wife, but came over immediately.

"This young man," he said, touching the back of my head, "has explained to me what occurred with a certain dog. Zasha, by name." Dimitri, the seasoned soldier, listened, giving away nothing by his expression.

"It was wrong of him to keep this information from us."

I felt my heart sink. "However, given that the dead man's identity is still a mystery, and the woman here today is not his wife, I believe I have a solution that will serve us all." I don't know who was listening more attentively, me or Dimitri.

"I would like Mikhail and his family to keep Zasha. There is no law to prevent it, and I . . . well, it's up to me to make decisions like this when there are no guidelines. Further, when she delivers her puppies, I want the Tarkov children to pick one puppy to keep. Assuming their mother approves, of course."

"Oh!" I gasped as his words sank in.

"But – I want all the other puppies to go to Dimitri to help him breed our new Russian dog."

"Thank you, sir," Dimitri said, standing at attention.

"Both of you understand that if we locate the family of the dead man, the dog will have to be returned to them."

"Yes, sir," we said in unison.

He seemed to relax for a moment because he said in a softer voice to Dimitri, "The boy said she's beautiful."

"Beyond words," Dimitri answered. "Her coat is like sable, her eyes—"

"The captain used to have a dog," I interrupted, hoping Dimitri would catch my meaning.

"As you know, sir, the dogs don't really belong to me.

They belong to the army. They are in my keeping for breeding purposes." A flicker of emotion passed over the captain's face. "But not all dogs breed well. We have only one female, not including any Zasha may give birth to." He hesitated. "What I'm saying is, at some point, the dogs won't be useful for the breeding programme and will need good homes. It's likely the army will leave those decisions up to me. I would be honoured to put you at the top of the list of recipients."

"I'm not making this decision to benefit myself."

"I know that," Dimitri said, "and I didn't mean to suggest it. It's my way of saying thank you."

I could see the captain was filled with thoughts and emotions and was struggling to stay in his role as police officer. "Dogs were our great helpers during the war. But the war is over now, and it's time to show our gratitude."

CHAPTER TWENTY FOUR

The front door practically flew open, and in ran Katia. "Where are they?" she cried. "Where are the dogs?"

No one answered. Finally the captain said, "How may I help you, Miss Klukova?"

She was out of breath from running. "I heard there were dogs. Lots of dogs."

In a kind but firm manner, the captain said, "How does this matter concern you, my dear?" I was still at the captain's side with Dimitri. We all walked towards her.

"Where are they?" She looked as though she would cry. Then, before any of us could speak, that's just what she did.

"Miss Klukova," the captain said gently, "whatever is the matter?" At first she shook her head and covered her eyes with her hands because it was impossible for her to speak. Finally, she looked up and took a deep breath.

"I just don't think I can stand it any more."

"Stand what?" The captain looked confused.

"Not having a dog. Not seeing a dog. Knowing" – and

here she caught herself from dissolving again into tears – "knowing I might never have a dog of my own again."

Remembering Rina's description of Katia's room as a "shrine" to dogs and seeing her so distraught helped me understand and even think about forgiving her for all her nosy, annoying actions in the last few weeks. "You mean you were just playing at being a reporter?" I said.

She practically whispered, "Not exactly. . ."

"You wanted to find out about a dog because you wanted one so much yourself," I continued.

"Yes." Katia sat down hard in a nearby chair as though her legs would no longer hold her. With the choked sound of tears in her voice, she said, "When I saw the hair on that man's coat, I just *knew* it was from a dog, or maybe I thought so because I wanted it to be true, I don't know. It made me sort of crazy. It was all I could think about, and talk about."

"And you were right," I said, with grudging admiration. "There was a dog." She looked up at me with eyes illuminated by happiness.

"All that talking almost resulted in harm to the dog," Dimitri said seriously. The light started to fade in her eyes.

"I never meant to. . . Is the dog all right?"

"She's fine," I said. "And if you hadn't been so talkative, maybe we wouldn't have caught the dog thieves."

By now, Irina, Nikolai, my mother and Rina had joined us to hear the conversation. Katia suddenly looked as pleased as if she'd caught them herself.

"And you actually caught them with the dogs?"

"At least ten, maybe twenty," I answered. She put her hand over her mouth and let out a muffled squeal of delight.

Looking sceptical, Dimitri said, "And what makes you care about dogs so much?"

"Mr Buttons. He was the dog we used to have. He taught me everything. How to be happy, how to be nice. How to love everyone. But he died. That was . . . so long ago." If she hadn't looked so upset, I might have made a joke about how it seemed she'd forgotten many of the lessons he'd taught her.

"Are you a hard worker?" Dimitri asked.

"Yes," Katia answered, looking confused.

"Are you willing to do the dirty work no one else wants to do?"

"Yes. . ."

"Then come to my kennel. I'll put you to work with my dogs." She jumped up from her chair and threw her arms around his waist.

"I'll do anything! Oh, thank you so much. You have no idea—"

"That's enough," he said, pushing her gently away from him. "Be there at six o'clock tomorrow morning. And wear your working boots."

"But . . . sir, ah, Dimitri, I would like the opportunity to work for you." Nikolai looked distraught that Katia would be there with the dogs and he wouldn't. "It was me, well, Mikhail and me, who trained Zasha. I think that experience gives me greater qualifications than Katia."

"Well said," Dimitri answered with a nod. "Just because the young lady will be helping me doesn't mean there isn't room for a fine young man like yourself. In fact, there will be so much to do once Zasha has her puppies, perhaps you and Mikhail would consent to assist me in their training."

"Fantastic!" I exclaimed.

"Yes, sir," Nikolai said. "We would be honoured."

"Any objections, Mrs Tarkov?" Dimitri asked my mother.

"I can spare them for the summer – assuming they get their chores done. Once school begins, they can help you only after their schoolwork is complete."

"That's fine, Mama," I said quickly. "We can do it all. Don't worry."

"What about me?" Rina asked mournfully, as we all started talking over one another in our excitement.

"Ah, yes." Dimitri got down on one knee so he could look Rina in the eye. "You didn't get to hear the news from the captain, did you?" She shook her head, still looking sad that she'd been left out. "Well," he said softly, "he said that your family may keep Zasha." Rina turned and leaned into my mother in her relief, clutching her skirt. "And. . ." Dimitri waited for her to look at him. ". . .he wants your family to have one of Zasha's puppies. With your mother's permission."

"Oh!" Rina flung herself into his arms. He held her and rocked her back and forth a few times before letting go.

We weren't the only happy ones. "Does this mean I won't be seeing you for a while?" Irina asked Katia with a half smile.

"Yes, madam. I hope I didn't trouble you too much."

Irina started to speak, as if she had plenty to say in answer to that statement, but then stopped herself and began again, perhaps remembering Katia's dad was still her boss.

"This might be the best story I ever write for the paper," Irina announced. "I want to get started on it right away. Can we go back to your house, Mrs Tarkov?"

I looked at my mother and my brother and my sister. "All right," my mother answered for us.

"Let's go now. I want to trace your steps from the time you met Petr . . . or whatever his name really was."

"Captain," Dimitri interjected, "I want to offer my services to care for the dogs that were recovered until we find their owners."

"Oh," the policeman said, looking upset. "I'd almost forgotten about those poor creatures in all the excitement."

"We need to get them out of those cages, give them food and water. I have plenty of room for them."

"Good idea. Those men aren't going anywhere until we sort this all out."

"Let's go, then!" Dimitri said. "Irina, why don't you ride in the jeep with me?"

Irina looked pleased, then said to the captain, "Mrs Gribovich's neighbour is waiting outside for her."

"Why don't you have him come in?"

"She said he's seen the inside of too many police stations! Would you or one of your officers escort her out?"

"My pleasure."

"I'll drive the van," Nikolai said, digging in his pocket for the keys.

"Can I go, too?" Katia asked with a hint of desperation.

"Of course. There's room in the van," Dimitri

answered. Nikolai didn't look too happy about this development, but didn't protest.

Irina sat up in front of the battered old jeep with Dimitri; Rina and I climbed in the back. Nikolai followed behind us with my mother, and Katia, and a truck full of dogs that had no idea that their moment of liberation was close at hand.

CHAPTER TWENTY FIVE

As we neared our farmhouse, Dimitri talked as excitedly as a child on Christmas Eve. "I saw a bulldog in there, I'm pretty sure," he said, talking about the dogs in the van. "He looked a lot like Mr Churchill – we'll call him Winston." He sped up to go around a hay cart. "I want to get those dogs out of their cages as soon as possible; they need water. Irina, why don't you come with me to the kennel? You can start your story there."

They looked at each other with "mischief in their eyes", as my grandmother used to say. Irina turned to look out of the window, trying to hide her smile.

"I can drive you back later," Dimitri continued. "You wouldn't want those poor dogs to suffer, would you?"

"What's that?" Rina asked, as Dimitri pulled off the main road and on to the access road to our farmhouse.

"It's an army transport," Dimitri answered in a tone so serious it frightened me. Parked directly in front of our house was a heavy-looking grey truck with a red star painted on its side and back. It looked bulletproof, and as though it had withstood the barrage of many bullets.

There was no one in the driver's seat, but I counted five men walking around the house as if looking for someone. We parked fifteen metres behind it; I turned to make sure Nikolai was with us.

"Let me do the talking," Dimitri said, in the same scary monotone. The three of us got out of the jeep and followed him. The soldiers, all in uniform, began quickly walking towards us. I heard my mother, Nikolai and Katia running up from behind.

The soldier who seemed to be in charge spoke. "We are looking for the Tarkov family."

"That's us. I am Mrs Tarkov," my mother said before Dimitri could say anything. I heard the fear in her voice.

"OK, men," he said. We all stood as if nailed to the ground as the men headed to the truck.

"What is this about?" Dimitri asked forcefully. "What do you want with the Tarkovs?"

The man didn't answer. He went to the back of the truck, which was remarkably similar to the one used by the dog thieves. His men followed him, silent and stone-faced. He paused before he opened the door, turned to my mother and said, "We have a delivery for you."

He opened the doors quickly. It took me a moment to

grasp what I was seeing. On each side of the truck was a bed, and on each bed lay a man. Both men were heavily bandaged.

"Constantin!" my mother cried. The bandaged figure on the right stirred. The soldier who'd opened the door now stood smiling as if this kind of surprise made him supremely happy.

"Just give us a little room, and we'll bring him out," he said. The other four soldiers entered the truck and unfastened the stretcher that lay on the bed so that the patient could be easily moved. The lead soldier folded down steps from the back bumper of the truck. We all backed up and made room for them.

Carefully, slowly, they moved the man I hoped was my father out of the truck. Once they were on the ground, we crowded around him.

"Papa, is it really you?" I said. His head was completely bandaged, covering his hair and wrapped twice around his chin. His right arm and left leg were both in plaster casts.

"Yes, Mikhail." To hear his voice after four years made me feel like a new person. It was all I could do not to hurl myself on to the stretcher and cover him with kisses.

My mother was at his side, holding his left hand, tears pouring from her eyes, saying, "Constantin, Constantin," between gasps of crying and laughing.

"Papa, it's me, Nikolai," my brother said. "Look how I've grown. I'll bet you don't recognize me."

Rina clung shyly to my mother. She had just turned five the last time she saw her father.

"Who is this beautiful girl?" he asked, smiling at her.

"Sergeant," said one of the men holding the stretcher, "where do you want him?" I'd barely noticed what a strain it must have been for them to stand there supporting a grown man.

"Oh," my mother said, as if she'd just realized it, too. "This way. Up the stairs." As they walked with their heavy load to the front of the house, I noticed Dimitri, Irina and Katia driving away quickly – he in the van, Irina and Katia in the jeep. I was disappointed to see them go without meeting my father, but could only conclude they wanted to give us privacy for our reunion.

CHAPTER TWENTY SIX

It wasn't easy for the men to carry my father up the stairs on the stretcher. "It's all right," my father said as one of the men lost his balance for a moment and they almost dropped him. "I can sort of walk if I can lean on someone."

"No, sir. Sorry, sir. These are the rules; we have to carry you into your house."

We'd all run ahead of them, and stood watching nervously from the top of the stairs. The door was open, and my mother was talking out loud to herself. "We'll put him in the front room. . . Oh, no, maybe we should put him upstairs, in our bedroom. . . Oh, the back room, that will be perfect."

My father made it easy for her by saying to the men, "Turn right, and then another quick right into the front room."

"Perfect, yes, of course," my mother said nervously. It was almost comical to see her so flustered after witnessing her strength and courage with the dog thieves.

"If you lay me on the sofa, you can get me into a sitting position, and your work will be done," my father instructed the men with a little laugh.

It was harder to do than it sounded, because the stretcher had to be taken out from under him. They finally managed it, but not without a stifled cry of pain from my father when one of the men accidentally bumped his casted right arm.

"Sorry, sir," the man said, touching the cast as if to reinforce his apology. The sergeant, who'd followed them in, stood proudly as my father adjusted himself on the cushions of the rose-coloured sofa.

"Are you comfortable, sir?" he asked my father.

My father sighed and looked slowly around the room. "I couldn't be better."

"We'll be going, then, sir. We've got another delivery." He saluted, as did the other men, and they went out quickly as we exchanged heartfelt goodbyes and wishes of good luck.

Rina sat at the opposite end of the sofa from my father, watching him, inching almost imperceptibly closer to him. My mother pulled a footstool from across the room on which my father could rest his left leg. His cast went from just above his ankle to seven or eight centimetres above his knee.

Nikolai placed a chair for my mother directly across from my father, and he stood behind it after she sat down. I sat on the floor gazing up at him, trying to make it real that my papa had returned from the war.

"Constantin," my mother said softly, reaching out for his free hand. "Can I make you some tea? Or get you something to eat?"

"Please, don't anyone move. I have dreamed about this moment since I left home." He looked intently at each one of us in turn, starting with my mother. His eyes fell last upon Rina. He patted the cushion on the sofa next to him. She shook her head no, but moved a bit closer to him.

"So," my father said, "what's new?" We laughed at the absurdity of his question, which I think is what he'd hoped for.

My mother was smiling and shaking her head back and forth, as if she couldn't believe that her dearest wish had come true.

"We didn't look away, Papa, not for anything," I said, remembering the words of the poem my mother had showed me. I could tell by the look of vulnerability that crossed his face that he knew exactly what I was referring to.

"And I came home," he said softly, paraphrasing one of the last lines of the poem.

"What happened to you?" Nikolai said, voicing the question on all of our minds. "Where have you been?"

"Look how you've grown, Nikolai," he said, seeming almost reluctant to answer the question. "Well, I'll tell you the details in the days ahead, but here it is, basically: I was in a German prison camp for a year and a half."

"Where?" I asked breathlessly, thinking of how he must have suffered in such a place.

"North of Berlin."

"Were you near the bombing?"

"Very."

"How did you get out?" Nikolai asked.

"Our camp was liberated in April."

"But it's July now. Why did it take so long to get you home?" I wanted to know.

"Why didn't you write to us?" Rina asked in a voice filled with pain, and a little touch of a reprimand.

"Well, my darling, even though they treated us badly in the camp, I was in one piece." I noticed he looked down when he spoke, as if he didn't want us to see something in his eyes.

"Then why didn't you write?" Rina asked again.

"Because your silly father almost stepped on a land mine!" He reached out, and this time she let him touch her hand.

"Almost?" Nikolai said. "Is that how you were hurt?"

He nodded slowly. "I was the lucky one. The two men walking in front of me died." All of us were silent, not knowing what to say. "I look much better now than I did after that, I assure you." He forced another smile. "And I remember things now that I forgot for a while."

"Did you forget us?"

"Not in my heart; only in my head. But then I remembered, and they patched me up and sent me home." My mother, who still sat transfixed in a kind of joy and disbelief, had tears streaming from her eyes.

I heard a sound no one else seemed to notice amid all the emotion and surprise – Dimitri's jeep pulling up in front of our house. I was certain I knew why it had returned. I stood up. "Papa, I have a surprise for you."

"You do? Do you want me to guess what it is?"

"No." I smiled and ran to the front door. At the bottom of the steps stood Dimitri and Zasha. I held my finger up to my lips so that Dimitri wouldn't say anything. He motioned his understanding and pointed to the jeep, indicating that he was leaving.

As softly as possible, I said, "Zasha, come."

She bounded up the steps, and I knelt down so I could hug and pet her. "You must be a very good girl," I whispered. "You're going to meet my papa." I tiptoed to the door of the front room, but held back just enough so no one could see me. "Are you ready?" I asked them loudly.

"Ready!" my father answered with a laugh in his voice.

Slowly and deliberately, Zasha and I entered the room and stopped. I wanted my father to see Zasha in all her beauty.

He let out a gasp of fear, and a look of terror crossed his face.

"Papa, what is it?" I cried, frozen to the spot.

"I . . . I. . . Where did you get that dog?" He was breathing heavily.

"She was with a man who came to the farm, but then he died." My happiness was quickly evaporating.

"It's a long story," my mother interjected.

"What's wrong, Papa? Don't you like her?"

He composed himself for a moment before he answered. "She's very beautiful," he said deliberately. "It's just that . . . there was a guard at the camp who had a dog very similar to this one." Then I understood. It was another example of how animals had been abused and misused during the war, only this example struck very close to home.

"Sit, Zasha," I said. "Lie down." She complied immediately, looking up at me curiously. I could see my father relax; he exhaled loudly.

"This is Zasha, Papa. And she isn't that dog." I was surprised by my own bluntness.

"She's very obedient," Nikolai added enthusiastically. "And we've taught her all sorts of tricks. She even sings!"

"And almost never barks!" Rina said.

"That's good," he responded. "That other dog never seemed to stop barking, and snarling, and. . ." His voice trailed off.

"Papa," I said, with all the strength and conviction I could muster, "if Zasha frightens you or brings back bad memories of your time as a prisoner, we will find a good home for her." I knew it had to be said. I also knew it had to be done if my father would be terrified at the very sight of her.

"What a man you've become," he said gently. "No, son, the war took many things from me. I can't let it take one more thing, certainly not the love of dogs. I can't live in fear."

"Are you sure?" My heart was so full of love for my father, I thought it might burst out of my chest.

"You say her name is Zasha?" I nodded. "Bring her a little closer."

"Come, Zasha." She walked with me to within a metre of my father. I could see him struggle with the memories that still possessed him. Then, without my saying a word, Zasha walked slowly up to my father and began to lick his left hand. He let her; and now it was his turn to cry.

"I'm sorry," he said, a laugh breaking through his tears. "I didn't cry during all my time in the army!" He stroked Zasha's head, and she came as near to him as she could, still licking his hand.

By that time we were all crying – with love, with relief, with gratitude. Through my tears I said, "I think today, the war is truly over."

THE BLACK RUSSIAN TERRIER

The story of Zasha, Mikhail and his family is a work of fiction. The effort to create a Russian "superdog" is based in fact, although it developed differently than in this story.

After the Second World War, which devastated the Soviet Union, there were almost no dogs left alive. Private dog breeders and kennels had vanished. Starvation, abandonment, illness, injury and service in the military had all but eliminated the rest. The Soviet government realized that it alone had the resources and ability to do something about the problem. A decision was made to create a new breed of dog, a hardy Russian dog, to be used primarily for working and military purposes.

Outside of Moscow at the Central School of Military Dog Breeding, more commonly know as the Red Star Kennel, the experiment began shortly after the end of the war. Most of the dogs were imported from territories occupied by Russian forces, especially East Germany. The few surviving breeds that could be found in Russia were also included. Under the direction of Colonel G. P. Medvedev, and with the assistance of Professor of Biology N. A. Iljin, the first dogs were mated.

The dog they hoped to produce would have several desired physical features and personality traits: a large, brave, strong dog – a hard worker, but one that was sociable and required minimum grooming. It had to be protective and smart, but they also wanted a loyal, calm canine that gave and needed affection.

Three breeds made huge contributions to these efforts: the giant schnauzer, the Rottweiler and the Airedale terrier. The Great Dane, the German shepherd, the Newfoundland and the Moscow water dog (now extinct) also played valuable roles. Although all the records from the government programme have never been officially released, enough information has been shared that it is known that well over a hundred dogs were used, and at least seventeen breeds.

By 1955, the Red Star Kennel felt confident that they had achieved their goal, and they presented the first generation of black Russian terriers to the public at the National Agricultural Exhibition. Everyone loved the dog immediately. In 1957, they began sharing black Russian terrier puppies with private breeders. Their popularity spread rapidly and to many nearby countries by the 1970s. The dog was nicknamed "the Black Pearl of Russia".

Today's black Russian terrier can weigh 35–70 kilograms and be as tall as 75 centimetres. His dense, black, wavy, waterproof coat gives him protection in the harshest climates. This dog loves to play with children, strives to please his master, is protective but nonaggressive, and needs lots and lots of exercise!

In 2004, the American Kennel Club gave the black Russian terrier official recognition in what is known as the Working Group. These dogs help their owners with tasks such as managing livestock, guarding property, pulling sleds and acting as rescue dogs on water and land. The passionate, but fictional, Dimitri Moravsky would have been proud.

ACKNOWLEDGEMENTS

To the Russian gentleman who proudly showed me a photograph of his black Russian terrier, telling me a few facts about its history, inspiring me to ask, "What if. . ." – thank you.

To literary agent Marlene Stringer, who believed in me long before *Saving Zasha* was born, I will always be grateful. Your warmth, wit and expertise have helped usher me into a new life.

To Jody Corbett, insightful, thoughtful editor, able to improve a manuscript in all kinds of amazing ways – I feel so lucky to have landed in your capable, creative hands.

Thanks also to editor Lisa Sandell for caring about *Saving Zasha* from the beginning. Your contribution during our time together made Zasha stronger.

A special thanks to my first and best reader, my mother, Dorothy Pitzer.

Finally, to my husband, Arthur. Without your support and encouragement, *Saving Zasha* could never have been written. Thank you for the space, and time, and believing in me.

ABOUT THE AUTHOR

Randi Barrow is a lawyer and amateur historian, who has also published adult nonfiction. When dogs entered her life a dozen years ago, the effect was profound. *Saving Zasha*, her first children's book, was inspired and informed by her canine friends. Now a full-time writer, she lives in Los Angeles with her husband, musician/composer Arthur Barrow, and their Chihuahua mix companion, Manuel.

If you enjoyed

Saving Zasha

you'll love . . .

All Hal ever wanted is a dog. . .

"Eva Ibbotson weaves a magic like no other.
Once enchanted, always enchanted"
MICHAEL MORPURGO

Every family has its secrets . . . ours more than most.

Grandad is getting worse. I try to cover up for him.
But last night, he could have killed us all. . .

Two boys lost in the frozen Finnish wastelands.
A girl searching for her missing mother. All three are lost.
All three face a desperate struggle to survive.

Part roaring adventure, part family drama, with a charm that's all Roddy Doyle.

"Roddy Doyle is an absolute genius!"
J. K. ROWLING